The Stone Soup Book
of Family Stories

The Stone Soup Book of

Stories

By the Young Writers of Stone Soup Magazine

Edited by
GERRY MANDEL, WILLIAM RUBEL,
and MICHAEL KING

•

Children's Art Foundation
Santa Cruz, California

The Stone Soup Book of Family Stories
Gerry Mandel, William Rubel, and Michael King, editors

Copyright © 2013 by the Children's Art Foundation

•

Stone Soup Magazine
Children's Art Foundation
P.O. Box 83
Santa Cruz, CA 95063

www.stonesoup.com

•

ISBN: 978-0-89409-030-1

Book design by Jim MacKenzie
Printed in the U.S.A.

Cover illustration by Emma Hoppough, age 13,
for "Bad Dinner," page 28

About Stone Soup

Stone Soup, the international magazine of stories, poems, and art by children, is published six times a year out of Santa Cruz, California. Founded in 1973, *Stone Soup* is known for its high editorial and design standards. The editors receive more than 10,000 submissions a year by children ages 8 to 13. Less than one percent of the work received is published. Every story and poem that appears in *Stone Soup* is remarkable, providing a window into the lives, thoughts, and creativity of children.

Stone Soup has published more writing and art by children than any other publisher. With our anthologies, we present some of the magazine's best stories in a new format, one designed to be enjoyed for a long time. Choose your favorite genre, or collect the whole set.

Contents

8 The Unfinished Jester
Emma T. Capps, 12

12 Mung Bean Noodles
and French Bread
Madelyne Xiao, 12

17 Sisters
Cameron Manor, 11

28 Bad Dinner
Adam Jacobs, 13

33 A Special Kind
of Family
Emily Boring, 13

36 Not Your Ordinary
Fairy Tale
Emmy J. X. Wong, 12

42 The Blueberry Family
Lena Greenberg, 11

49 Breaching the Wall
Jonathan Morris, 13

54 A Different Kind
of Light
Catherine Babikian, 12

57 Ashie
Rie Maeda, 13

65 The Strawberry
Olympics
Ryan Gallof, 13

69 Rescue
Mailyn Fidler, 13

71 The Dragon Speaks
Emmy J. X. Wong, 11

78 JuJu
Natalie Schuman, 11

82 The Summer
Father Was Away
Sariel Hana Friedman, 10

86 The Forgotten Fort
Andrew Lee, 13

91 Saturdays
Sophie Stid, 13

96 Zachary
Adanma Raymond, 12

98 A Long Way
from Home
Emily Livaudais, 11

102 A Different Kind
of Lullaby
Meg Bradley, 13

107 Love—A Cursed
Blessing
Akash Viswanath Mehta, 10

114 The Old Farmhouse
Shannon Halpin, 12

117 A Faraway Place
Emmy J. X. Wong, 11

122 The Animal Kingdom
Mackenzie Hollister, 12

127 The Garden
Emma Agnew, 13

130 Roaring Regret
Michael Scognamiglio, 13

133 Not Ready
Aubrey Lawrence, 12

The Unfinished Jester

by Emma T. Capps, age 12

IN MEMORIAM. Angelo Salvatore D'Amico, 1919–1989. That was what I wrote, at the bottom of the painting, in felt-tip pen. That isn't the beginning of this story. It's the end.

This story starts a month earlier. It starts in the library.

That's a room in our house—the library. Right next to my bedroom, across the hall. It's filled head to toe with books upon books, stories upon stories. In one corner is a tall fireplace, near the couch and the faded leather armchair. On the mantle are Halloween pictures of me: kindergarten, third grade, fourth grade, sixth grade. On a different shelf are old black-and-white photographs, grainy and lovely, of my mother's parents.

My mother and I were sitting on the rug, flipping through black portfolios she had put together of my paintings and sketches. She was proud of her work. I was proud of her work.

"See, Emma?" she said. "I've put all your drawings in these plastic covers, so they don't get faded. Look—there's that watercolor you did of the girl and the calla lilies."

Emma was living in San Carlos, California, when her story appeared in the May/June 2010 issue of Stone Soup.

"Thanks," I said. "You did a really nice job with these portfolios. Why is this one backed with newspaper?"

"I don't know," she said, shrugging. She flipped the portfolio page.

"That's amazing! Who drew that?"

She had flipped to a breathtaking charcoal sketch on yellowed old paper. It showed a dark, meticulously drawn little house teetering on a cliff above a lake. The drawing was gorgeous.

"My dad made it," she said wistfully. "You remember I told you he loved drawing?"

"He was very skilled," I said.

"Yes, well," she said sadly, "he never got to use his skills."

"Why not?" I asked, although I half knew the answer.

"He had to work all the time to support our family. He never had time to be an artist."

I flipped the page. It was a portrait of a man, his sculptured face dark and brooding. His long hair was pulled back in a ponytail, and he wore a fancy coat with tails and a ruffled cravat.

I didn't like this drawing as much as I liked the first drawing. On the next page was a third drawing, and this was the most captivating of them all.

It was a black-and-white charcoal portrait of a court jester. His face was spread in mischievous delight, his snub nose upturned. In his right hand, he held a staff with a toy face on top, almost a mirror of his own. He wore a voluptuous coat and pants, decorated with thin outlines of birds and stars, moons and tiny trees. The detail on the coat seemed unfinished, as did his left hand. The hand was a mere outline, pale and ghostly.

My mother and I stared at the picture.

"I never realized he didn't finish this picture. Look at the left hand and the coat. I think he was drawing this right before he died."

"It's beautiful," I said. "*My* paintings pale in comparison."

"No, they don't," she said seriously. "You're already a better artist than he was."

"Do you think he would be proud of me?" I said, smiling slightly.

"Yes," she said. "He would be extraordinarily proud of you."

"Would he help me with my art?"

"Yes. I don't think you need it, though."

We sat there for a long time.

"He was a good man," she said, tears brimming in her eyes.

MY GRANDFATHER DIED a long time ago, when my mother was eighteen. On our mantle, right there in the library, is my mother's favorite photograph of him. He's smiling from ear to ear, wearing his Navy-issue baseball jersey and throwing his glove into the air after his team's victory. Even though the photograph had been taken during his service in World War II, his face is nothing but pure joy.

So he played baseball. He drew. And I wish I had known him.

TWO DAYS LATER, I took the court jester out of the portfolio. I brought him over to my drawing table, cleared a place of honor for the drawing among my desk clutter, sketches, and art supplies. I tore a sheet of paper from my watercolor pad, got out my best mechanical pencil, and began to draw. I stared at my grandfather's court jester and copied him carefully. I refined the lines, finished his left hand and drew in the details on his coat, carefully penciled in tiny stars and birds and trees.

I inked it in. I did this all in secret, when my parents weren't watching. I didn't want them to know. This was between me and my grandfather.

Then I painted it. In watercolors, because they were my favorite medium, rich and versatile. The jester came alive, and my grandfather did too. My grandfather came alive through my pencil, my pen, my paintbrush. He smiled out through the court jester's lips.

I stood back and stared at my grandfather's jester, my jester. It had been a month since I first saw the sketch. Homework and school and life had crowded out the jester, but whenever I had a moment I inked a little here, painted a little there. Now it was finished, and it was beautiful.

No—not *quite* finished. Not yet.

"Mama, what was your dad's name?" I called out.

"Angelo. Why?" she yelled back, sounding puzzled.

"Just wondering!" I said.

I pulled out a felt-tip pen and wrote my In Memoriam at the bottom of the painting.

"There," I said. "*Now* it's finished."

Then I went out and played baseball. I threw much better than usual. I think my grandfather was throwing through me.

Mung Bean Noodles and French Bread

by Madelyne Xiao, age 12

"HERE," MY MOM shouted in Mandarin over the bubbling of the cooking pot. She lifted her hand and motioned me over.

"Hold on to the handle," she grunted, nodding to the handle of the slowly revolving pot as she stirred with a pair of chopsticks.

I chuckled. "I'm guessing that the bottom of the pot isn't flat?"

Mom lifted the pot up ever so slightly and glanced at the convex surface. A stray drop of boiling water dripped from the spatula onto the glass cooktop and sizzled dry.

"Affirmative."

I gingerly held the handle while Mom scurried over to the counter and brought back a bowl of fine white powder. I sniffed, and smiled. The evanescent fragrance of mung bean wafted out soothingly.

Mom now held the bowl, poised at the cooking pot edge. The boiling water purred below the bowl's lip.

"Ready?" Mom inquired, half teasing, half serious.

Madelyne was living in San Carlos, California, when her story appeared in the May/June 2010 issue of Stone Soup.

THE STONE SOUP BOOK

"Yawp," I rolled my eyes, but still instinctively blinked as I heard the first dusty sounds of powder sliding on powder, then the wet "plop" of collision between powder and hot water. The burning spray of water that I always half expected never came.

Humming one of my piano pieces, Mom went about stirring the cloudy mixture, pushing her hair out of her eyes as she worked. There was a certain comfort in watching the apron-clad figure prepare one of our family's favorite dishes, accompanied by a Chopin waltz.

"Ouch," she suddenly gasped. The chopsticks stopped their revolution around the pot's inside and clattered to a halt on the pot's rim. Her stirring hand flew up to her mouth, and she quickly sucked on the tiny burn that had been caused by the pop of a bubble of hot mung bean water.

"Lemme see," I clamored, tugging childishly at Mom's tightly clutched hand. She reluctantly pulled away her hand to reveal a small, teardrop-shaped burn that blushed a rosy pink. Mom carefully extricated her hand.

"It's OK," she reassured. "It's not the first time." I knew that she was in a rush—Dad was coming home from a business meeting in Paris in half an hour, and everything had to be perfect. Still, I thought I could see her wince as she grasped the chopsticks again.

Hoping to be helpful, I wandered over to the dish rack and plucked out a large, long-handled bamboo spoon.

"Mom, use…" I started.

She shook her head automatically.

"Stay away from the stove—it's really hot now, so if the bubble pops, you're going to get a burn twice as bad as this little blemish," she nodded at her hand.

By now, the cloudy white water had thickened to a paste in the pot. There was the thick *thlop!* of boiling air bubbles as the sweet-smelling concoction simmered and burped like some sort of Yellowstone mud pot.

Mom had, by now, turned off the stove and was rinsing her

hands in cold water at the sink. She exhaled slowly and grimaced. It was then that I noticed the odd speckling of pinkish burns along the back of her hands.

"Your hands really got burned," I exclaimed stupidly. She gave me a sideways glare.

"Thanks for stating the fact," she chuckled, shaking her head. "My hands feel much better already."

Mom checked the clock. Twenty minutes, and Dad would be back home. She pressed the surface of the cooling mung bean paste with her hand. I half expected her fingers to sink into the agonizingly hot starch, but her knuckles merely brushed the translucent surface. The paste quivered slightly, like Jell-O, but held firm. Lifting the pot up slowly, Mom pried the block of paste out with a pair of chopsticks and let the pot-shaped block relax into a plastic bowl. As usual, I was amazed. The bottom of the pot looked as if nobody had used it in the first place, and the curved surface of the paste block was flawlessly smooth. Mom smiled at her handiwork.

"Beautiful," she finally decided.

I contented myself with sitting at one of the bar stools by the counter, listening to the muffled tapping of Mom's knife slicing easily through the soft gel and meeting the solidity of the cutting board. I half dozed, listening to the soft *tap-tap* of the knife, the rustle of the tree leaves outside, and the sound of a car motor.

My eyes shot open.

A car motor?

I raced through the living room to a front window, where the already raised blinds revealed the sight of a large, black Lincoln Town Car that squatted in the driveway.

"Mo-om!" I screamed. "Dad's home!"

"Greet him for me. I've got to season this stuff," she scowled at the bowl of mung bean starch noodles that she'd cut the block into.

Slipping on a pair of sandals, I pelted outside, to where the cab driver was helping Dad unload. Dad stopped and smiled.

THE STONE SOUP BOOK

"Bonjour, mademoiselle?" he laughed and gave me a hug. Once the bags had been put in the shoe room and the taxi driver paid, I turned to Dad.

"So, how's Paris?"

"Beautiful place. It's old, but the atmosphere's fantastic," he responded. "You and your mom would love it there."

"How was the food?" I spat out the question that I'd been dying to ask for a week.

Dad brightened. "Wonderfully light. Of course, it doesn't compare to your mother's cooking. Speaking of which…" He grinned impishly and raised his eyebrows.

I stood by, watching, as Mom and Dad hugged and smiled, with Dad rushing back to his suitcase for the gifts he'd brought us. Besides a snow globe and keychain, he set another oblong package down by two bags of French chocolate.

"Here, hon. I got something for you that I hope you'll like. Open it!" It was a command. I opened the package's carefully folded waxed-paper wrapping and smiled. Dad had brought me a real French baguette. My mind automatically snapped to what my French teacher had told me at school. French bread was special—no preservatives, with a thick crust that hid a soft, fluffy inside. A gourmand in the making, I'd obviously blabbed about baguette to my dad the day I'd learned about it. It was something that was nearly impossible to come by in America. Instinctively, I stuck my nose into the wrapping and sniffed deeply, then smiled. The sweet aroma of wheat was as good as that of mung bean.

"Aw, Dad, you shouldn't have," I exclaimed, thinking about the absurdity of flying a loaf of bread cross-Atlantic.

"Well then, you don't even have to eat it," Dad laughed. "Just look at it, if that's what you want."

"Not eat it? What a waste. Of course we'll eat it," came the hasty reply.

Dad shrugged. "I hope it's worth it. I had to go through such a fiasco getting that loaf through customs." He rolled his eyes. "Mysteriously wrapped oblong package, eh? In fact, they wanted me to eat a piece to see if it was tainted or not!"

As I watched Mom and Dad prepare the rest of dinner, an irrepressible feeling of happiness swept over me. I smiled at the sight of Mom and Dad preparing dinner together for the first time after a week. I smiled at Mom's gentle chiding as she reprimanded Dad for cutting the cucumber too thin. I smiled as I heard the familiar sounds of appreciation as my mom finally approved of Dad's cucumber cuts and went on to pester him with questions on how many euros he'd spent buying our gifts. Not a lot, Dad would reassure her.

I thought of the distances love for our family could go. Halfway across the world for a loaf of bread. A handful of burns and half an hour for the tired traveler's favorite dish.

As we sat down to eat dinner that night, I laughed inwardly at the inquisitive surprise on my mom's face as she took in my ear-to-ear grin. After all, she laughingly told me later, Dad had only been away for a week.

Sisters

by Cameron Manor, age 11

1. Our Magical Island

"HEY, CAM," MaCall whispered, nudging me in the side to wake up.

"What?" I asked groggily, peeling one eye open. "What time is it?"

"Midnight," MaCall grinned.

I groaned.

"I got some M&Ms from the vending machine at gymnastics. Do you want to share them with me on a magical island?" MaCall asked excitedly.

"Huh?" I moaned.

"A magical island—*the roof!*" MaCall whispered, her green eyes lighting up. "Now go get these jeans and tennis shoes on—I don't want you to get hurt in case you fall off!" MaCall urged, thrusting clothes at me.

Yawning, I pulled them on.

Cameron was living in Laguna Hills, California, when her story appeared in the March/April 2010 issue of Stone Soup.

"Put this belt on too," MaCall commanded, handing me a pink sparkly belt. "I'm also wearing one. We'll attach another one between us so we can be like mountain climbers," MaCall explained, hurriedly tying my belt while she double-knotted hers.

"Uh... shouldn't we tie mine tighter?" I asked, looking doubtfully at my mountain-climbing getup.

"Don't worry about it. You're lighter than I am," MaCall sniffed, tossing her blond hair over her shoulder. "Wait. Let me just make sure Mom and Dad are asleep. You stay here."

MaCall tiptoed over to our parents' room and placed her ear to the door as I sat there fuming. MaCall thinks she's stealthier than I am, but the truth is, she's downright noisy. Every time we sneak downstairs to "get a glass of water," (i.e., eat ice cream and watch our favorite late-night TV show), she either creaks every stair or topples down the whole flight with a giant *BANG* that would wake the dead. Well I guess the last thing is kind of my fault. I kind of advised her that the faster you move, the quieter you go, but now I see it depends on who's going.

"Definitely snoring," MaCall announced cheerfully, beckoning for me to follow her. "Well Cam, are you ready?" she asked, quietly opening her bedroom window. (It's the only one in the house with a removable screen.)

"Yes," I snorted with all the pride an eight-year-old could muster.

"Yo. Don't snort at me like that. I'm thirteen years old. You're lucky I'm bringing you on this adventure!" MaCall whispered, looking all offended.

MaCall pushed me out the window and onto the wood-shingled roof that slanted below it.

"Ouch, MaCall!" I screeched, trying to pry the splinter out of my hand.

"Now stay there, I'm coming out!" MaCall announced.

Two seconds later, she had plopped down beside me.

"Whoops!" she cried as she almost slipped on a loose shingle.

"If Dad knew about this, he would be so mad!" MaCall said, calmly ripping open her bag of M&Ms and pouring them into her mouth.

"Oh yeah. Here," she said, handing me one brown M&M.

"Oh gee, thanks," I said, crunching down my one M&M.

"You're welcome!" MaCall said cheerfully, silently enjoying her bag of M&Ms.

To tell you the truth, I was getting a bit bored.

"Do you have any more candy?" I asked hopefully.

"I'm not a vending machine," MaCall said dryly.

"MaCall, can we go back now?" I asked hopefully.

"No."

A car's headlights suddenly shone against our house.

"*Duck!*" MaCall screeched, diving to hide her head between her arms.

Personally, I don't think it helped much. I looked at my sister and sighed.

"MaCall, I don't feel like I'm on a magical island. I feel like I'm watching you eat M&Ms," I moaned, watching her scarf down the last one.

"What? You mean you're not at this very moment burying your toes in hot sizzling sand as the sun sinks into the sea?" MaCall whispered, closing her eyes and sprawling back on the splintery shingles with a contented sigh.

"No."

"Well then... *use your imagination!*" MaCall screeched, then clapped her hand over her mouth. "Do you think Mom and Dad heard that?"

"Yes," I whispered, closing my eyes and grinning. "Even a deaf person would."

"Huh. Then maybe we should go back now," MaCall said hurriedly, scrambling to her feet. "Wouldn't want to get grounded for the next 300 years."

MaCall reached out a hand to me and looked at me with mischief in her bright green eyes. I reached out my hand to clasp hers, and at that moment, I knew she was my sister.

2. My Sister the Spy

"HEY, CAM, guess what?" MaCall giggled.

"What?" I groaned, knowing this meant trouble.

"I made us these files for our 'agency,'" MaCall chirped, slapping down a manila folder with a mysterious number 52 on it.

"Did you steal these from Dad's office?" I asked, looking at them suspiciously.

"Yeah, well that is not the topic," MaCall said breezily. "The topic is that *we are starting our own spy agency.*"

"Oh."

"Aren't you excited?" MaCall breathed, her eyes practically popping out of her head.

"Uh, the thing is, MaCall... whenever we do something together, I usually get in trouble."

MaCall looked offended. "Name five times that happened."

"Well, there was that one time that you convinced me to eat candy on the roof with you because it was a magical island and then dad found the wrappers when he was hanging the Christmas lights."

"Umm—that's *one,*" MaCall shrugged in disgust.

"And then there was the time you hid your stray cat in my closet and Dad thought it was *my* cat."

"Well..." MaCall hemmed.

"...after which Dad made us knock on *every door in the neighborhood* to ask if they had lost a cat—which was really embarrassing."

"That was last year," MaCall said, rolling her eyes.

"And then you're always making me play *Naiads...* " I began.

"I object to the word 'always,'" MaCall interrupted.

"Dad yelled at us for three hours for that!"

"It's not every day you can pretend you're a water nymph and steal your little brothers' souls," MaCall said smugly.

"Also, just recently you gave me five dollars to buy you a drink and a brownie and it ended up costing $6.25..."

"How was I supposed to know it would be that expensive?" MaCall protested.

"It was really embarrassing because there was a long line of people staring at me," I harrumphed. "And then there was... *huh*," I hesitated, trying to remember the long list of injustices I had endured over the years.

"That's *four* things," MaCall said, her eyes bright with triumph.

"There've been so many things it's hard to remember," I protested.

"Mom and Dad won't even hear about this," MaCall murmured, pulling out her cool wax seal kit.

I squirmed uncertainly.

"Fine! I'll just be a spy by myself then," MaCall shrugged, flouncing off.

"OK, I'll be a spy with you!" I shouted.

"Great!" MaCall cried, whipping around and looking delighted. "Your first mission is..."

"But I'll only be a spy with you under one condition," I interjected.

"And what is that?" MaCall moaned.

"If we get in trouble you have to tell Mom and Dad it was your idea!" I declared.

"What-*ever*, can you just sign this contract?" MaCall groaned, shoving a sheet of paper in my face.

"I promise to be a spy with MaCall," I read aloud. *"Signed, Cameron Manor."*

"Now write your name on the bottom line," MaCall ordered, pointing at the blank line.

"OK," I replied, scribbling in my best cursive.

"Great! Now we must seal the envelope," MaCall announced, lighting the red candle in her wax seal kit and dripping the wax all over the envelope.

"Aren't you supposed to drip the wax into a circle?" I asked, feeling confused.

"Yeah, but this way makes it look prettier," MaCall grinned, stamping it with her M for MaCall signet ring and burning the edges for a finishing touch.

"Girls, what are you doing?" Dad asked, sticking his head in the room and sniffing suspiciously. "What's that smell?"

"What smell?" MaCall asked innocently, shoving the evidence in my drawer.

"What are you two even doing?" Dad asked, marching into the room to find out for himself.

Dad yanked open the door to find a burned manila envelope with red wax dripped all over it.

"Girls! Just what do you think you're doing?" Dad yelled, slamming the drawer shut with a bang. *"You could've burned the whole house down!"*

"Sorry," MaCall shrugged.

"MaCall, don't you have something to tell Dad?" I asked.

"No, I don't think so," MaCall said, turning away.

"Girls, I don't want to see you doing this again unless Mom or I give you permission," Dad said sternly, stalking off sighing.

"OK, now let's get back to business," MaCall said, sighing with relief.

"What? Are you kidding me!" I screeched.

"Uh... no," MaCall answered.

"Did you hear what Dad just said?" I asked.

"Yeah, a good spy is not put off easily," MaCall said. "Besides, you signed the contract."

"Fine, but..."

"Great! Time for your first mission. You may open the envelope now," MaCall said in a hoity-toity voice, waving her hand in the air like a princess.

"Whatever, but if I get in any more trouble..."

MaCall just rolled her eyes.

I opened the envelope. Here is what it said:

To: Agent Grover
From: Agent Smuff
Mission: Go borrow $20 from Mom's purse
Reward: When one agent helps another, that agent will be helped

"What is that supposed to mean?" I asked.

"Uh... what do you think? *Go steal $20 from Mom's purse!*" Ma-Call screeched, getting red in the face.

"OK!" I roared back.

I tiptoed off to my Mom's room, only to find that she was *sleeping with her purse!*

"*Pssst...* Cameron, get over here," MaCall whispered.

"What do you want now?" I asked, tiptoeing back where Ma-Call was poking her head out from behind the door.

"I forgot to tell you... good luck, Grover," MaCall grinned, winking at me.

"*Am I free to go now?*" I asked impatiently, tapping my toes.

"Yes."

I sighed and tiptoed back to the room where my mother was sleeping, unaware of the drama that was unfolding two inches from her nose. Heart pounding, I carefully lifted her arm and slipped her purse out. Quickly, I snatched a $20 bill from her worn brown leather wallet, put everything back the way it was, and dashed out of the room.

"Here you go, Agent Smuff. Mission *accomplished,*" I sighed, tossing the $20 bill at my sister.

MaCall looked at the bill.

"Uh uh uh!" MaCall *tsked* disapprovingly. "I recall saying '$40 dollars.'"

"You mean I have to go in there again?" I asked, horrified.

"Yes, you must... you have not completed your mission, Agent Grover," Agent Smuff snapped, green eyes flashing.

"OK fine, but this is the last mission," I said angrily, stalking off.

MaCall just grinned.

THE NEXT DAY, MaCall returned from her rhythmic gymnastic convention with a new ribbon stick, new ribbon, new clubs, new tape, and a new ball.

"Well, I guess you gotta help *me* now," I observed politely, eyeing all her new stuff.

"What is it you want?" MaCall asked in her nicest tone. She was in a really good mood because she had just gotten everything she wanted.

"A new MP3 player!" I answered without hesitation. It was only $20 (which I knew because my sister had just gotten one), so I thought it was a fair trade.

Agent Smuff looked shocked.

"What are you *thinking?* I can't just go out and buy you that kind of stuff!" MaCall screeched.

"But you said, 'when one agent helps another, that agent will be helped,'" I said, remembering my contract.

"Yeah, hmmm…" my sister muttered distractedly, disappearing into her room.

And that was the end of the agency.

3. My Sister's Garage Sale

"I KNOW HOW much you love boxes, Cam," the sticky note read.

I stared at three battered boxes that didn't even close properly. Probably my sister hadn't wanted to lug them down to the garbage can, so she had "gifted" them to me. I sighed and lugged them to the corner of my room, where they sagged on top of the rest of her "presents."

I am my sister's beneficiary, the one upon whom she lavishes gifts. Two-inch pencil stubs, old discolored nail polish, broken jewelry where the beads fall off and the clasps don't clasp, stained sticky notes with only two sheets left, books that don't "look good" in her room—all these treasures are mine for the enjoying.

I think what it really is, is that she can't be bothered to walk down the stairs, so she uses my room as a garbage dump.

One day I decided to speak up.

"MaCall, I just don't want your trash," I said politely, delicately placing a year's worth of MaCall's gifts back in her room.

"That's not trash... those are my gifts!"MaCall cried, her eyes wounded.

I stood there, trying to be firm.

"*Caaammm!*"—*sniff sniff*—How c-could you?" MaCall wailed.

It's actually kind of funny to watch teenagers cry, 'cause every once in a while you can see a smile poke out through their tears. I cleared my throat and threw my shoulders back, trying to remember the speech I had prepared.

"MaCall, for the past year I have been collecting your 'gifts,' and I don't want them anymore!" I screeched, stalking out of the room to take a hot shower to cool off.

When I returned, MaCall was sprawled on my bed, muttering in her sleep. (For some reason I scored the best mattress in the house, and MaCall knows it. Also, MaCall doesn't like making her own bed, so she sleeps in mine.)

I poked her.

"MaCall, can I have my bed back?" I asked politely.

"Mom, don't wake me up! I can't do that right now..." MaCall groaned through a cobweb of dreams.

With a sigh, I plopped onto MaCall's bed and fell asleep.

"*What is going on? I never said you could sleep in here!*" MaCall screeched, catapulting me out of her bed with one swoop.

"Um, MaCall—you were in *my* bed. Where else was I supposed to sleep?" I pointed out, rubbing my butt.

MaCall glared at me, then flounced off.

Two minutes later, she was back.

"I am really sorry about what happened. Will you forgive me?" MaCall asked, green eyes wide and as calm as a kitten.

"OK fine," I muttered, wondering what she was up to now.

"Well... would you like to buy some special scratch paper? It's five cents for twenty sheets," MaCall asked brightly.

I looked at the sheaf of papers MaCall had thrust at me. Basically, it was the blank backsides of MaCall's old homework that she had sprayed with Sweet Pea perfume.

"Uhhh…" I hesitated.

"You don't like the scent? I also carry them in La Poison," MaCall chirped, her eyes lighting up.

"I'll stick with Sweet Pea," I answered, handing over a nickel.

When it comes to MaCall, don't even bother to resist. It's better to do just whatever's on her mind.

MaCall smiled.

"Thank you for your business. Now would you care to look at the other items I have for sale?" MaCall said brightly, shoving the nickel in her pocket.

Before I could answer, MaCall waved her hand over an elaborate display of old pencils, dirty eraser pieces, Elmo hair scrunchies we had last worn when we were five years old, plastic necklaces whose "diamonds" had long fallen off, and…

"MaCall!" I screeched, snatching up my favorite frog pajamas that were now curiously… shorts.

"Yes?" MaCall asked innocently.

"What did you do to my favorite frog pajamas?!" I screeched, clutching them to my chest.

"I had no idea those were yours," MaCall huffed. "Anyway, they look much better now."

I stalked out of MaCall's room, furious. MaCall was always cutting up her clothes in an attempt to be a fashion designer, but cutting up my favorite frog pajamas was going a bit too far.

"It's artistic!" MaCall called out desperately.

I pressed my hands over my ears, trying to shut her out.

What I really need, I thought, is a little sister. Someone I could dress up, tell advice to, give stuff…

"Hey, Jack!" I called out to my six-year-old brother as he bent over the carpet to draw an eye patch on his pirate.

"What do you want?" Jack muttered, looking up at me in annoyance. Jack hates to be interrupted, but this was an emergency.

THE STONE SOUP BOOK

"Would you like to buy some special scratch paper?" I asked brightly. "Just five cents for twenty sheets."

"What do you mean by 'special?'" Jack asked curiously, looking up at me with a gap where his tooth should have been.

"Uhhh... they smell really good," I answered, thrusting the sheets under his nose.

"I'll pass," Jack said, returning to his pirate drawing.

Oh dear. I think I'm just not cut out for sales.

Bad Dinner

by Adam Jacobs, age 13

W E'RE EATING CHINESE tonight. Dark plastic bowls filled with rice and vegetables, egg rolls in little cardboard boxes, even the fortune cookies with the lottery numbers on the back of the paper. This is a real treat. Mom doesn't care for Chinese food, but it's Dad's favorite, so tonight she's putting up with it. In case you hadn't guessed, I kind of like it, too. I crammed about six pieces of sweet-and-sour chicken in my mouth and smiled at Mom. She forced herself to smile back. I could tell she wasn't into the food tonight.

Dad reached his hand across the table. Mom placed her hand over his, stroking it gently. I've never seen them do that before. "Jason," said Mom, "you love your father, don't you?"

"Um... of course. Why?"

"And your father loves you more than anything else in the world," Mom continued. Dad nodded his head. "He wants you to grow up to be the best that you can be."

"Mom?"

Adam was living in Brooklyn Park, Minnesota, when his story appeared in the November/December 2009 issue of Stone Soup.

THE STONE SOUP BOOK

"But sometimes, when you grow up, you have to make decisions that aren't... easy." I could tell Mom was softening things up. But what was she getting at? Did I do something bad? Was there something wrong with Dad? Were they getting a divorce? I mean, they fight sometimes, but I never thought... "Your dad wishes there were more options, but sometimes there just aren't."

"Mom, please spit it out." I couldn't take it anymore. I thought this was going to be a great night. We ordered Chinese. The weather was getting nice. I was thinking about seeing a movie.

"Jason, your father's job is being moved to California."

I stared at Dad. He looked back at me, his eyes deep and soft. "You mean Dad's out of a job?" I asked.

"No, it's not like that. He's going to California, too."

"Wait! We're coming with, right?"

Dad looked sadder than I had seen him in years. He shook his head slowly, once to the left and once to the right. That's when I realized what was actually happening.

"Wait, why? Why do we have to stay here? I want to go with Dad!"

Dad swallowed and cleared his throat. "I wish there were another way, Jason, and if there was I would do it, but these are very difficult times and we *need* the money."

"Why can't Mom find a job?"

"There are *millions* of qualified people out there looking for work. We can't take that chance," Mom said. She put her hand on my shoulder. "I know we'll all miss having Dad around. But don't worry! He'll call us every night, and he'll still fly up here on holidays. Besides, it's only until we pay off the house."

"That's not the same! Why can't we just live off of welfare or something? We could get by! Isn't it worth it if we can keep Dad here?" I could hear myself getting angry before I knew it.

"We'd have to give up the house, which is bad because we owe more than it's worth. We'd sell most of the furniture. We'd live in a small, dusty apartment in a bad neighborhood. We'd use food stamps and thrift stores to get by."

"So? You guys can handle that!" My voice quivered.

"It's not about us. It's about what's best for you."

I just about choked on a piece of chicken. "For me? It'd be best for me to have my mom and my dad in the same place!" Rice sputtered out of my mouth and stuck to the table. There was a moment of pause. Mom tilted her head to the floor, gripping Dad's hand tightly. I saw a tear rolling down her cheek. I felt guilty. Did I make her cry? Was she just sad that Dad's leaving? It felt a little unfair at the same time. It wasn't *my* fault that Dad was going away. Then I had another thought. "Dad, do you think they'll change their mind?"

"What do you mean?"

"Do you think if you ask real nice, they'll let you…" I trailed off because I felt stupid saying it, but I really *wished…*

"I already asked. They're very sorry."

That was the moment where it all felt real. There was no other way. It was going to happen. Mom and Dad just stared.

I stood up and left the table. I didn't know what I was going to do, I just thought, *I need to get away, I need to get away.* It was a stress-relief type thing. Sometimes I have to hit a pillow to get it all out. A pillow wasn't good enough, though. Pillows are soft and fluffy. I could feel a panic setting in, but I didn't know where it was coming from. I spun around. I felt like screaming, but that wasn't much better than a pillow. I spun until I got too dizzy. Then I did something stupid.

I ran out the door as fast as I could. I didn't have any shoes. It was dark. It was *so* cold. The stress kept building up inside of me so I ran faster and faster, but it was no good. I thought about what my life would be like with Dad gone. He was always *there* for me. He drove me places. He gave me advice. He could talk to me about… I don't know, girls and stuff. I *need* that kind of support. In first grade, we learned the difference between needs and wants. Dad is a *need.* Money is a *want.*

I yelled at the top of my lungs, even though I knew it wasn't enough. My feet hurt really bad, but I didn't care. I thought about

THE STONE SOUP BOOK

running forever and never coming back. I thought a lot of crazy things that I won't admit. My chest heaved in and out, forcing me to sprint faster. I couldn't see much, just dark rows of houses, and the road going out ahead of me. Miles and miles of suburban wasteland. I wanted to go away from the houses. Houses reminded me of home, and that's the last place I wanted to be.

I DECIDED to stop at the gas station. A guy in the back looked at me funny, but he didn't say anything. People at gas stations don't really care about much. Get your snacks. Gas up. Go. I forgot why I stopped here. Maybe I was just cold. I looked down at the tile. I could almost see my reflection, if it weren't for the cracks in it. Gas stations are really depressing. I guess I fit right in.

I walked to the back of the snacks aisle and knocked on the bathroom door. No reply. I walked in and sat down on the only toilet, resting my face in my hands. I imagined how hard it must be for kids who only knew one parent. Was it more difficult if you had a chance to know them first? That thought only got me more depressed, and I looked around for something to take my mind off of things. Four walls. Lots of little tiles. Water on the floor under a tiny sink. I ripped off a square of toilet paper to make myself feel better. Then I ripped off another, just for the sake of it. I kept ripping until there was a huge pile of paper waste on the floor and the roll was almost gone.

I shoved them into the trash bin and walked back to the snack aisle. It felt good to waste stuff sometimes. I was tempted to throw some of the snacks in the trash, but then the store clerk would get mad at me. I could tell I was getting bored. Here I was, spinning my wheels at a gas station while my real problems were miles away back home.

I thought about my parents. I'd been gone for a few hours. They'd be worried about me. Maybe they were looking for me. I stumbled outside. There was a truck pulling away. I didn't like the way it smelled. I wished I could do something about it. I wish a lot of things. None of them would make that truck stop smelling.

I plugged my nose instead.

I started thinking about Dad again. He loved me. I couldn't help that he was going away, but maybe if I plugged my nose… OK, bad analogy. But the thought got my brain working again. I didn't want Dad to feel bad. I wanted to make him proud, and I wanted him to be happy again. He was probably ripping his hair out now, trying to figure out where I was. I turned back towards home and ran.

I JOGGED BACK through my neighborhood. It was way past my curfew. All of the houses were dark. It was a welcoming environment. A couple of cars drove past me. I hoped it was no one I knew. I'm guessing I looked like a mess. My ears were freezing off, yet I was sweating at the same time. One of the cars turned on some extra lights. They were blue and red. "Hey!" yelled the cop. "Is your name Jason?"

Oh great. "Yeah."

"Are you eighteen?"

That's a weird question. I was tempted to say yes, but I suppose messing with a cop is a bad idea. "Not really."

"All right, get in the car, Jason. Let's get you home." I opened the back door. It was heavier than I expected. Or I was tired. I buckled myself in behind the driver. There was a wire mesh to separate us. I felt like a criminal. In light of that, I decided to ignore him if he said anything else. I have the right to remain silent.

We drove the remaining two blocks to the only house with lights on. The officer walked me to the door. He rang the bell and we waited. I snuck a peek at him. He looked pretty bored. He's probably looking for some extra cash, too, being out this late picking up kids. I hope someone pays him for bringing me home, even if it was only two blocks. I heard footsteps from inside and more lights flipped on. They rushed to the entryway. I knew who it would be. The door opened. I gave Dad a hug.

A Special Kind of Family

by Emily Boring, age 13

Our car trundled along a dusty gravel road one day in the middle of July. I stared out the window at the clouds of dry dirt that billowed from beneath our tires, picturing what our car must look like from the outside. Aside from the layer of dust covering it, our big red Subaru looked completely normal. With two kids in the back seat and a trunk filled with towels, bags, and blow-up water toys, our car was the image of an ideal family headed off for a fun summer day. I sighed.

I wonder what it would be like to have a normal family. How different would life be if Aaron were an average ten-year-old boy? I pondered. I knew that if anyone looked past our car and surveyed the people within, they would not find an ideal family. They would see that my younger brother has autism. They would see that, at age ten, he can't do certain simple things like dress himself, read, or talk in full sentences. And they would see how much Aaron's special needs keep our family from being perfectly normal.

Emily was living in Salem, Oregon, when her story appeared in the March/April 2010 issue of Stone Soup.

After a few more miles, our car crunched to a stop in a dusty parking lot, and my train of thought was interrupted as I climbed out of the hot back seat. I was relieved to be back at the lake that my family travels to every summer for a day of swimming. It looked just as I remembered it, a small green lake nestled into a wooded hillside. I inhaled the spicy scents of sagebrush and pine, wafting from the central Oregon vegetation. As I exhaled, glad to be back in this beautiful setting, thoughts of my family's imperfections were momentarily wiped from my mind.

Emerging from the car behind me, Aaron let out a joyful yell, exclaiming "Oh! Oh yes!!!" He then picked up a nearby stick and attempted to hit a pinecone with it, pretending to play baseball. He associates baseball with happiness and does not hesitate to grab a makeshift ball and bat whenever he is pleased. Embarrassed with his behavior, I grabbed my towel and ran down to the rocky lakeshore.

I immediately plunged into the chilly water, frolicking around and shouting that everyone should hurry up. It was a sweltering day, and the lake was dotted with other swimmers, many in the vicinity staring at Aaron, who was still playing "baseball." Upon reaching the point where ripples of water lapped up against the pebbly ground, my dad plodded slowly in, punctuating each step with a loud "Ow!" as the icy water made contact with his skin. Aaron tried to run right in but forgot to take off his shoes, shirt, and glasses. After my mom removed them, he proceeded with painstaking care until, with an enormous splash, he lost his footing and fell chest-deep in water. Finally my mom, who has a notoriously low tolerance for cold water, screwed up her courage and dove under.

We took off swimming—Aaron swims with a peculiar dog paddle—until we reached the very heart of the lake, where huge white driftwood logs floated and provided nature's best toy. I pulled myself up onto one, noticing how pale and eerie my feet looked as they kicked a few feet below the surface. Aaron struggled for a moment to pull himself up on the log, the difficulty of this

THE STONE SOUP BOOK

simple action reminding me how much his disability affects his coordination. I took pity on him and helped hoist him up.

Exhausted from his efforts, Aaron collapsed on the log and pushed his sopping brown hair out of his eyes. Suddenly remembering last year, he exclaimed, "Jump!" Upon his command, I sprang off the slippery wood and dove into the water, causing the log to rock and create a sea of ripples. Following my example, my mom jumped off, and my dad helped Aaron to fall off the log in an uncoordinated dive.

After dozens of crazy, log-rocking, water-spraying jumps, many involving disastrous attempts at cannonball contests and synchronized diving, we finally took a rest. My mom stretched out on the sunlit log, and my dad sat next to her. We were all lost in the moment, a whirl of happiness and fun that warmed us as much as the late afternoon sun did. Aaron, perched a few feet down the log, patted the wet patch of wood beside him, smiling proudly as though he offered the coziest chair in the world. "Sit! Come sit!" he invited me.

I climbed closer to him, and together we sat. My feet dangled in the cool green water and I listened contentedly to the buzzing of millions of pine needles tingling in the forest. My nose took in the wilderness-like, sunny smell of the setting. We were just a family sitting on a log in the middle of a lake. My family.

And in a dawn of realization, it occurred to me that I had just spent the last hour completely enjoying my family just the way we are. Anyone looking on wouldn't think about how strange and different Aaron is. They would have seen how happy we were, they would have been caught up in the joy and fun we had been radiating. It seemed to me in that moment that nothing, not even perfection, could match the happiness, spontaneity, and love that makes my family unique.

Overcome by my new thoughts, I scooted even closer to my brother, and together we gazed at our reflections in the green lake. The image of our smiling faces was bent a little by the water, but the imperfection made us look all the better.

Not Your Ordinary Fairy Tale

by Emmy J. X. Wong, age 12

EVERY DAY was a holiday, or so it seemed. You didn't need decorated trees, fireworks, cakes and candles, or paper hats to celebrate special days, Marty thought. Marty loved her lazy Sunday mornings perched on a high stool in her galley kitchen, eating stacks of buckwheat pancakes dripping in amber syrup, lovingly cooked just the way she liked 'em, crispy brown on the outside and fluffy golden yellow on the inside. Her dad had promised that Sundays were their own special days together and no one would ever interfere. She loved her dad for that and for the myriad of special days he had devoted to her. She savored every one of them. She loved regular Friday-night barbecues on the geranium-lined terrace just as much as the sailing vacations on Martha's Vineyard that only came each windswept August along with the humidity.

Of all her favorite days, her most favorite ones weren't vacation holidays at all, but ordinary afternoons figure skating at the Frog Pond across from their Beacon Hill brownstone on

Emmy was living in Weston, Massachusetts, when her story appeared in the September/October 2009 issue of Stone Soup.

THE STONE SOUP BOOK

late wintry afternoons, just as the sun was sinking. The magenta-and-plum sky, reflecting in the shimmering raspberry-blue ice, mixed together like oil pastels to create magical vistas. With the row of cupolas standing guard on the hill, just beyond the iron fence surrounding the Common, the Boston skyline was right out of a medieval fairy-tale picture book. She had become a princess, and her dad her knight in shining armor. With him protecting her heart she felt safe in a world that had slung more than a few arrows at her.

Until Jessica arrived. After Mom died, it had been just the two of them. That was nine years ago. She had been almost four years old, then. Dad always said no one could take Mom's place and Marty knew deep down that she could believe him; he was trustworthy. No one could possibly ever take Mom's place. Marty still had fuzzy memories of her broad cheerful smile, and floral scent, her sparkly eyes and the polonaises she loved playing on the baby grand. There were signs of her everywhere in the apartment. Dad kept their wedding photo on display on the Steinway in the great room and a bottle of her favorite gardenia scent on his dresser. But Jessica now seemed like a constant interloper. She just showed up one day and never left, sort of like Marmalade, the orangey-red striped tabby who arrived on their doorstep in a blizzard and adopted the modest-sized family on the spot. She had unabashedly come knocking at the door in need of a cozy home and constant scratching behind her ear, and Marty had been overly eager to pamper her. Now she owned the place. Jessica in a similar way had wedged herself in. Jessica had been sent over by her dad's publisher. He was an experienced writer and she a young aspiring editor who wanted to throw herself into her work—and *Marty's world*, brimming with rainbows.

MARTY LOOKED DOWN at the carefully scripted aqua "J" intertwined with "S" for Sinclair on the back of the envelope that held the engraved wedding invitation. It sat royally now on the mahogany sideboard biding its time. Sinclair Roberts.

Ever since she could remember, she envisioned that one day she would grow up and leave the nest first, not the other way around.

Marty Roberts. Although everyone mistook her for a boy, with her short cropped fiery red hair, and a uniform of cutoffs and perennial rocker T-shirts, she thought *she* would be the one to break up the pair eventually as she sped off to an all-girls' college or maybe even—marriage to her own Prince Charming. Never in her wildest fantasies did she think her dad would be the one to break up the duo. But Jessica had other plans and dreams for herself, which selfishly included Dad. Marty gasped for air. Suddenly, she felt all her memories and her future slipping out from under her like quicksand. Her happiest days were behind her for certain.

"Honey, come in here." It was Dad, chirping from the living room with all the brightness of a spring robin. "We need you!"

I wonder, Marty pondered skeptically.

When Marty entered the large sunlit brick front room with the sheer muslin curtains, Dad and Jessie were hand-in-hand on their favorite spots on the couch. Marmalade was spread out across Dad's lap, licking one paw, enjoying a midmorning bath. Why was it Marmalade had no trouble staking her rightful claim to him, when she had so much difficulty? Marty smiled at the placid feline, which resembled a carefree dust rag in an indulgent pose. She wasn't going to be displaced from her castle—by anyone. Marmalade purred contentedly.

"Marty, which of these party favors do you like best?" Jessica pointed to a glossy brochure, one of several opened before the blissful couple. "Your dad likes these miniature porcelain swans filled with pastel butter mints. But they seem so old-fashioned to me. I need your help. I like these Belgian-chocolate swans in colorful tinfoil." Both looked hideous to Marty.

Marty searched for a diplomatic answer. She would prefer neither. She would prefer that Jessica go away and that there would be no wedding, but that wasn't a choice the pair of entangled arms and hearts had given her. Marty could see why her dad liked Jessica. She wasn't a stunning beauty. She was more the "girl next door." Pretty and nice enough. Jessica continued to carry on a dialogue to fill the void.

"Are you OK with the wedding, Marty? Do you want us to wait until you graduate from eighth grade next summer? We can wait, you know. I realize it's just been you and your dad for some time. If you need more time to get used to the idea, we can give you all the time you need." Her voice had become steady and low, one might even say reassuring and understanding.

There she goes again, thought Marty. It's true. As much as she resented her, Jessica was all right. She always said the right thing at just the right time. She knew why Dad had, OK, admit it, fallen in love with her and she knew why she was having so much trouble disliking her. Jessica was a kind person. She was smart and maybe even beautiful and she made it a point to spend as much time with *her* as she did with Dad. Marty remembered how she took her and two friends shopping and to lunch on Newbury Street to celebrate her twelfth birthday. When her dad was reluctant to buy her the expensive cell phone she wanted, Jessica went to bat and enumerated all the ways she was responsible.

"Marty does all her homework, is always where she says she is and has never given you any cause to worry about her. Of course she can handle a new cell phone. She needs it. She won't lose it or allow it to get stolen. I have no doubt," she had argued intelligently. Her dad appreciated logic and, as a best-selling author, recognized a plot when he heard one. Of course, the two had ganged up on him and had rehearsed it ahead of time. It was two against one. Now it was the other way around.

Marty pulled up a chair and decided to try to get used to the idea of her dad's marriage to Jessica. Her world though seemed to be churning again, like the bottom of the ocean futilely trying to brace itself for a hurricane motoring up the coastline in full fury. She had enjoyed a few good years of stability, but now it seemed stormy days were eager to flood in again; the clouds were beginning to take shape overhead. Soon, Jessica and Dad would be on their honeymoon in Bermuda and she would be all alone, in search of a silver lining to all those clouds or, better yet, one last rainbow; at least Marmalade needed her. What would happen when Jessica became her stepmom? Would she suddenly sprout a wart at the tip of her nose, or turn out to be a twin to Cinderella's wicked stepmother? That's how the familiar story went.

ONE DAY TUMBLED into the next and soon the day that put her into a panic each time she thought about it had finally arrived. Marty was glad that this day had finally come. This was the climax to the story. This was the one part she was now ready for after so much contemplation. What she wasn't certain about was its ending. In many well-loved fairy tales, Prince Charming rides in for the last few pages, but after all, I'm only twelve-and-a-half, thought Marty. "No, I'm afraid there isn't going to be a fairy-tale ending for me," sighed Marty with a heavy heart.

The picturesque whitewashed chapel with the pointy steeple came into view sooner than she had anticipated. Marty could hear the familiar organ march sailing out softly on a breeze as soft as butterfly wings. Outside the church, a wave of bridesmaids in frosted aqua blue, pink and lilac dresses, the color of beach glass, waited in attendance under a brilliant sky. But once inside, Marty felt the air still and turn stifling. The sea of navy and black suits, paisley ties and flowery dresses wearing oversized hats seemed to swallow up all the oxygen and she felt she was drowning.

She felt so uncomfortable and awkward in her cornflower-blue empire-waist gown, making her way down the aisle now, hoping someone would throw her a life jacket. Her thoughts floated away to earlier in the day when her grandmother had painstakingly tried to make a chignon out of her tuft of orange hair she had tried to grow out specifically for the wedding. But all her efforts seemed to be in vain as the wisps escaped the tightly pinned bun at the nape of her neck. Everything seemed to be falling apart. In front of her, now Jessica and Dad held hands. Marty hadn't seen her Dad look this happy since—since she couldn't remember when.

Marty tried to catch her breath. "I'll just try to fade into the woodwork," she whispered to herself, "or maybe melt into the pine floorboards and pretend to be invisible." Her heart was shattering into a million pieces, by the reflective twinkle in Jessica's eyes, lovingly gazing back at her father.

But just then, her dad and Jess dropped their hands and opened their circle, extending their arms out to her. "Martina," her dad called to her in that rich, baritone, soothing voice she knew so well. Jessica then called out without hesitation, motioning to her, "Marty." Marty didn't know what to think. They both wanted her to join them at the foot of the altar.

"Marty, will you take us to be your new family?" her dad asked in earnest.

"Marty, will you accept me into your life as someone who loves you and cares about you?" questioned Jessica imploringly, with honest eyes, putting her arms tightly around her waist.

"Oh yes, yes!" Marty heard herself venture, but in only broken words in a cacophony of sound—because she was sobbing so loudly.

"YOU SEE, it wasn't *just* your ordinary fairy-tale ending," Marty suggested to the passenger sitting next to her, hanging on every word, racing toward pristine pink beaches and high-flying skies together. *"It was so much better than that!"*

The Blueberry Family

by Lena Greenberg, age 11

TWO GIRLS SAT on a small, colorful carpet in the living room of their new house. The older one, a lanky seven-year-old redhead, sat up tall and poised, her feet tucked underneath her. The younger one, a chubby four-year-old with brown curls, was sprawled out on her stomach, paper dolls scattered around her.

"Allie, play with me?" the little girl, Jessie, said. She was tired of all the moving boxes, and her parents' distraction. Unfortunately, her parents loved moving and did it frequently, due to both their work, their spirit for adventure, and restlessness. But playing with her sister, the gorgeous, poised Allison, would make up for it.

Allison smiled. "OK. Do you want to play with these paper dolls or with the new game Mommy brought us?"

The little girl scrunched up her face in concentration. "Paper dolls," she decided.

"OK," Allison said. "Now, who do you want to be?"

"It's a family," Jessie said. "I'm the oldest child, um... Andrea."

Lena was living in Philadelphia, Pennsylvania, when her story appeared in the March/April 2009 issue of Stone Soup.

THE STONE SOUP BOOK

Allison giggled. "And I'm the youngest child, Jenna. What's their last name?"

"Um... Blueberry!" Jessie said, remembering the fresh, sweet berries they had tasted when they lived in Maine.

Allison sighed. "That isn't a real name. What about... Smith or something?"

"No. Blueberry," Jessie said, still able to savor the sweet berry.

"OK, Blueberry it is."

And so the Blueberry Family was born.

I KNEEL ON the hardwood floor, peering into a moving box with the set of paper dolls we used as the Blueberry Family. Allison and I are helping unpack in our new Connecticut home. I take out the packet of paper dolls and smile as I hold it up to Allison.

"Hey Allison, remember these?" I call out, but Allison continues unpacking. Silent. I sigh and look down at the packet. I had actually never forgotten the Blueberry Family, where I was the bossy older sister and Allison the cute younger sister. Allison and I shared a brilliant imagination despite our three-year age difference. The story we made up was magical: in the Blueberry Family's world, Jenna and Andrea lived at a magic amusement park near a blueberry field with their parents. At night, after everyone had left the park, the Blueberry Family tried out all the rides and even slept on the Ferris wheel. Sometimes Allison would draw pictures, illustrating our Blueberry Family stories. The Blueberry Family kept me stable through all our moves.

"Allison?" I say again, louder. "Remember the Blueberry Family? Maybe we could play with them again one of these days? Hey, remember that one story we played with them when the merry-go-round..."

She sighs. "Look, Jessie, I liked playing with you and everything, but we're older now and I think we need to find our own friends."

I feel numb with hurt.

True, I had seen it coming. The graceful, poised, child Allison has grown into an outgoing, social fifteen-year-old Allison, who isn't interested in me. Once I had adored her, and that felt special, now it seems everyone adores her. Allison gets better and better at making friends, while I continually struggle to find just one. Worst of all, she's too old for magic amusement parks and paper-doll families.

One of the things I used to admire in Allison was her unique way of thinking, so unlike all the other kids her age. When she was nine, she told me that she never believed in magic as in flying, but magic as in friendship. Even as a six-year-old I recognized the wisdom and sophistication of the statement. But she hasn't said anything like that for a while.

I leave the room. She doesn't seem to notice.

"Jessica?" My mom looks over the staircase to see me. "Look at this house, Jessica. Can't you just feel the spirit?" She takes a deep breath.

I don't respond.

"No? Well, you will, soon enough. There's everything we need here. This is a wonderful town. This is where we'll stay."

Even though she says that every time, it gives me a boost just to hear it. Maybe Connecticut will be different. Maybe I'll find lots of friends here, more than Allison. Maybe I'll find a secret door leading to a magic amusement park... I'm not too old for those kinds of dreams.

"Donna, you can't promise that," my father says, stepping over a moving box. The living room is cluttered with them.

"Why not?" she demands.

"Because of my job, and besides, that's just the way we are," Dad says.

I sigh and edge back up the stairs.

O N THE FIRST day of school, I decide to bike there instead of taking the bus. I want to be away from the prying eyes of children who tease newcomers.

"So I'll see you later," I say to Allison as I take my cereal bowl to the sink.

"Mhmm," she says.

"Maybe later we could play, um, do something together?"

She stands up, almost knocking her chair to the floor. "Jessie, I'm going to the mall with Lucille after school. I don't think there'll be time for that today."

"Who's Lucille?"

"Oh, you haven't met her yet? She has a sister just about your age, I think. She lives across the street," Allison points, "and she's the coolest."

"Right," I say vaguely. I miss the days before "coolest" became part of Allison's vocabulary.

"Jessie, you need to get going. School starts at 8:20," says Mom. She looks out the window and sighs. "Look at this town. We're staying here, Jessie."

"Humph," Dad says.

"Well, we are!" Mom cries.

"It's best not to get their hopes up, Donna."

"What's wrong with getting their hopes up?" Mom asks. Both of them have forgotten that Allison and I are in the kitchen too. I look at Allison, hoping to share an eye-roll, but she looks out the window.

WEARING MY BACKPACK, I dash up the old oak tree right outside our house and find a comfortable spot.

No one seemed to see me as I introduced myself in class, ate at an empty lunch table, and sat alone at recess. If we move again soon, away from this school district, I won't mind.

While I do my homework, I see Allison cross the street to a car in front of Lucille's. I see her jump in the car, laughing and smiling, her jovial voice carrying across the yard. I see the car drive down the road, and, after about an hour, I see it come back. I climb down the tree and wait for Allison to finish waving and calling out to Lucille about future trips, et cetera, et cetera. Then

I plant myself in front of her as she walks towards the house.

"Can we do something now, Allison?" I know better than to use the word "play."

She drops her three plastic clothing store bags, her eyes glinting with anger. "You know what your problem is, Jessica Taylor? Well, I'll tell you. You need to get a life instead of clinging to me for support all the time. You need to have friends your own age, who like normal things instead of weird amusement parks. You need to grow up. You're always holding onto what we did as kids!"

I glare at her and notice her golden earrings, swaying in the breeze.

"If you want to make friends here, Jessie, start out somewhere that isn't blueberry families."

I blink back tears. I just can't let go of seven-year-old Allison, so willing and patient to give up her normal name of Smith for Blueberry.

That isn't the Allison who stands before me, shopping bags at her feet.

"I've stopped caring now, Allison," I say, surprised to hear how harsh my voice is. "Everything I once admired in you is gone. You aren't what you used to be." I turn and walk inside the house.

A LLISON AND I don't speak to each other for over a week. Every time I see her, I feel a pang of regret for my outburst—I don't want to lose her—and a pang of anger—how could she change so much?

School doesn't get any better. No one notices me, not even Lucille's sister, the one my age.

But my teacher, Ms. Carolyn, is nice. She gave us each a private journal to write in over the course of the year. I like to fill mine with my poems. It relaxes me. I hand in some of the poems for creative writing assignments, and they usually get A-pluses. Ms. Carolyn has also assigned a project for her class this year: to choose from a list of jobs to help around the school. I've volunteered to help with the younger kids in the after-school program. It's a fun job. The little kids' make-believe games are entertaining. Whenever I watch them, I think of Allison, and our fight, and the Blueberry Family.

ONE DAY ALLISON leaves early for school. She and Lucille want to do something together before school starts. I don't know what and I don't really want to know, either.

As I am leaving, Mom calls out to me. "Jessie, Allison left her lunch here. Can you please take it to her?"

"Sure, Mom," I say.

But inside I worry. What will Allison say when I approach her?

At my elementary school, I lean my bike against a wall and look out at the many kids: running, shouting, giggling, chatting. Across the street, at the high school, I spot Allison with her friends. She still has her beautiful red hair and her poise.

I look back at the kids at my schoolyard.

I see some kindergartners and imagine how they will grow up, change, and become high-schoolers across the street. And I remember what Allison said: "You're always holding onto what we did as kids." But I can't let those things go. We move so much. Everything changes around me. What's wrong with holding on?

Warily, I cross the street and approach Allison.

"...so I decided to use soft tones here." Allison holds open her sketchbook. She still draws?

"Allison?"

She almost drops her sketchbook.

"Y-you forgot this," I say, showing her the lunch bag. She puts away her sketchbook and takes it. I walk away.

"Wait—Jessie?"

"What?"

"I need to talk to you—in private," Allison says.

I look over at her friends.

"Oh, everyone, can I just say something to my sister here?" Allison asks.

"Sure," Lucille says, as Allison leads me around the bend, away from her friends.

"Um—what's this about, Allison?" I ask, looking at the ground, at the jungle gym across the street, at my sneakers.

"Well, I'm sorry, Jessie."

I look at her.

"I'm sorry that I've been kind of harsh with you," Allison continues. "I just wanted to help you."

"Oh," I say. "Well, I'm sorry too."

She raises her eyebrows.

"Maybe you were right," I say. "Maybe I am holding onto the Blueberry Family too much. But don't change so much, Allison. You're the only friend I have!"

"I was trying to help you find new ones," Allison says. "I love you, Jessie, but I need to leave behind the stuff we did as kids. You do too. It will help you find friends."

"But I don't want to change," I said.

"I don't think we ever completely change," Allison says. "I think we just… take what we used to love to a different stage. You have a wonderful imagination, Jessie. You'll always have it. But you can use it in different, more mature ways. I hear you're doing well with your writing assignments—maybe you'll be a writer."

I can't help but smile. Allison hasn't lost her wisdom after all.

"Thanks for lunch," she says, and smiles back. "You're a great sister."

"So are you," I say.

"Well, see you around, I guess," she says, and walks over to her friends. Squinting just a little, I can picture her kneeling on the floor, paper doll in hand. Then I open my eyes. I don't need to see her as a seven-year-old anymore. That was then. This is now.

Breaching the Wall

by Jonathan Morris, age 13

THERE STOOD GRANDPA Wilson, his old yet strong form slightly hunched over, while his gaze followed our car as we pulled up to the house. The light drizzle dripped off the old tweed cap he liked to wear. As I clambered out of the car, a grin app eared on his face and he opened his arms to hug me. As I wrapped my arms around him, I could feel his red woolen sweater scratching my skin. A few moments later, Mom appeared with little Betsy. My little sister charged Grandpa and allowed herself to be picked up in his strong arms and smothered with affection. "Come in, come in," said Grandpa. "Grandma's been hard at work all morning baking cookies for you."

"Yum, yum, yum!" shouted Betsy, who had immediately lost interest in Grandpa and desperately tried to get out of Grandpa's arms and inside to the cookies.

Inside the scent of homemade chocolate-chip cookies filled the air. "Hello," shouted Grandma from the kitchen. "Who wants cookies?"

Jonathan was living in Grantham, New Hampshire, when his story appeared in the January/February 2009 issue of Stone Soup.

"*Meeeeee!*" yelled Betsy at the top of her lungs. A few moments later, we were in the kitchen, stuffing ourselves with cookies. Betsy elaborated on and on about how tedious the car ride to Connecticut was. When I looked up from the vast plate of cookies, I noticed that Grandpa had disappeared.

I knew that Grandpa was the kind of man who realized that arguing with his wife is pointless and for the most part avoided her by pursuing his interests—reading World War II stories and biographies of infamous criminals in the hut by the brook and repairing furniture and building bookshelves for his ever-expanding library in his workshop. I also knew that he didn't like spending time with other people. Still, stunned that he would leave us the moment we arrived, I inquired about his whereabouts.

"He's probably in his workshop; he's got a bookshelf that he's got to finish," answered Grandma.

"Why don't you go and build something with him? He always wanted to make a model boat," suggested Mom.

I walked down the hallway, turned at the open door and peered down the stairs to Grandpa's workshop. I could hear a paintbrush swishing over wood. I walked silently down the stairs and watched Grandpa staining the individual boards of the bookshelf. The evilly toxic smell of the wood stain flooded my nostrils and almost made me gag.

Finally, he finished and set the pieces to dry. As Grandpa turned, he noticed me, sitting on the unfinished wooden stairs. "Well, hello Peter," he mumbled, "what brings you down here?"

"Mom said we should make a model boat together," I stated awkwardly. "If you want to," I added. Grandpa said nothing. He went over to the corner of the shop, mumbled to himself a bit and then appeared with several two-foot-long boards. I just stood there, not knowing what to do.

"Come on, let's get to work," he ordered. We took the boards and cut them into thinner strips. Then, we started making the ribs of the boat.

We worked until dinner in almost complete wordlessness. The Grandpa who had welcomed us was long gone; this new silent Grandpa seemed here to stay. As I went to bed, I made a wish that the old Grandpa would come back.

The next morning, we were working on the boat bright and early. Around eleven o'clock, Grandpa was using the lathe to make the mast, and the wood molded perfectly under his chisel. When the mast was complete, he turned the lathe off and took the wood off of the spikes that held it in place. He started talking, loudly enough for me to hear but not looking directly at me. "What shall we call her?" He looked up after a moment and I grasped that he was asking me. I thought for a moment and then stated, "The *Seadog*, the dreaded ship of Pirate Captain Wilson."

"And don't forget his loyal first mate, the swashbuckling Peg Leg Peter," he added, showing a seemingly uncharacteristic smile. "They sail the high seas, robbing rich merchant ships and giving to the poor."

Grandpa seemed to have let a bit of himself out and I realized that Grandpa wasn't the boring old man he seemed to be. Just then, Grandma called down that lunch was ready and we headed upstairs for our midday repast. After a delicious meal of grilled cheese with juicy tomatoes and smoked ham, we were back at work.

Now Grandpa seemed to be more open, although he didn't say a word. While fitting a miniature royal yard to the main mast, he spoke excitedly. "The *Seadog* is the fastest, most maneuverable, best crewed ship on the high seas."

"And its crew is wanted by all the merchants in the known world," I continued.

"Why she once fought the *Endeavor*, flagship of the East India Tea Company, and came out victorious," Grandpa explained authoritatively. "The freedom-fighting duo of Captain Wilson and Peg Leg Peter boarded and captured Blackbeard's ship single-handedly." As he spoke, he fit rigging to the already besailed masts. "Recently, though," continued Grandpa, "the *Seadog* was forced to fight an entire column of British ships-of-the-line led by the *HMS Victory* herself. The *Seadog* suffered grievous losses but she will sail again someday." At first it seemed as if his story was done, but as he attached a miniature pirate flag to the flag-staff, he made as if to say one more thing. "I believe, that day is today!"

He picked up the finished boat and impishly motioned for me to follow him as he bore our precious cargo to the brook. I peered into the gurgling waters and worried for the *Seadog* on her maiden voyage. "Wish her luck," smiled Grandpa, setting our beloved model into the water. As she floated and bobbed along, we followed her trek.

Suddenly, she sped up. "Oh no! The falls!" Grandpa exclaimed. The thought of having our work destroyed quickened our pace, but it soon became apparent that we would not reach her in time. As he watched her sail over the edge, our pace slowed and we slid down the small ledge to see what could be salvaged.

As I looked up from the treacherous rocky scree, I saw the *Seadog*, completely unharmed, run aground on the large, flat river stones. Relieved that the boat was intact, we brought it back to the house, laughing about our good fortune. That evening, Mom and Grandma were surprised by how Grandpa talked and laughed with me. I had breached the wall of Grandpa's self-induced solitude, a seemingly impossible task, the same way the *Seadog* had braved the waterfall.

After that fateful day, Grandpa remained really open around me; he even associated with others a bit, which caught everyone off guard. When it came time to leave, I felt truly sad to go, but I knew it wouldn't be long before I returned.

Later

I WALKED THROUGH the door that seemed infinitely more familiar since that time my eight-year-old self had really gotten to know Grandpa.

"Hey, Grandpa," I shouted as I shrugged my rain-soaked sweatshirt off.

"Peter! So good to see you," he said, with the ecstatic emotion of a child on Christmas morning. "Boy, have I got the book for you, a biography of Al Capone. It's one of my new favorites." He hobbled off toward the library, motioning for me to follow.

As we entered the cluttered room, I noticed a model boat sitting atop a shelf.

"The *Seadog*," I remembered.

A knavish grin appeared on Grandpa's face as his shaking hands, showing signs of his developing Parkinson's disease, picked up the boat. "What do you say? I think Captain Wilson and Peg Leg Peter will sail the *Seadog* again."

"One last time," I finished.

A Different Kind of Light

by Catherine Babikian, age 12

AMY RAN. She ran and ran and ran and ran because she never wanted to stop. She flew past churches and office buildings, the sound of her Nikes crushing the gravel guiding her. Her muscles didn't hurt; her skin was simply a garment she could peel off when she got hot. Amy wanted to get as far away from that building as she could get. The smell still permeated her nostrils and she ran harder, ran faster, as if the closer she was to home the faster she could get rid of the smell. Sweat dripped down her back, nestled itself in the crevices of her face, but she didn't care.

Amy ran faster. Never had she run like this before, but she found that the more she thought, the more she wanted to go home, the farther her legs would take her.

Running was a mental sport, Amy decided.

Amy did not slow down for several miles. How far away was she from that hospital, that place she never wanted to see again? Seven miles, she reasoned. She approximated the route at thirteen miles, which seemed reasonable, so she would have about

Catherine was living in West Des Moines, Iowa, when her story appeared in the September/October 2008 issue of Stone Soup.

six to go. On any other day, Amy would be intimidated, but not today, not when all she wanted to do was go home. Away from that hospital, which reeked of antiseptic and sick people, away from her father, who couldn't say two words to her, away from the nurses and doctors all in white, who fake-smiled at Amy while secretly feeling sorry for her. Forty-five minutes, give or take, she'd be home. Home.

The image of her mother flashed in her mind as she ran, becoming more vivid and then suddenly blurry in a flash; she found that she had to probe her mind to find the good images of her, not the ones where her mother was small and frail, but the energetic woman Amy knew her to be. A twinge of guilt stabbed her heart, letting misery flow through her veins; it took extra energy to keep running now. She had been selfish, uncaring. She had left the room in a hurry, wishing she would never have to go back, despite the calls from her father. Her mother had even called her name, whispered three words down the hall, where they floated in her ears, but she had not turned around.

Amy wished she had. She had heard the words—I love you— but she had not responded to them. Amy had not cried, although anguish was pouring out of her in buckets. And Amy knew that the way to rid herself of the permanent melancholy that had overtaken her was to cry, but she never cried. She had stopped crying a long time ago.

Four miles to go. Amy pulled her watch up to her face; she had forgotten to wear her glasses that day. Nine twenty-four. The little display glowed in the darkness, the only light she could see that was not a streetlight. The moon wasn't even out to guide her... her mother loved full moons, she thought. But Amy pushed the thought out of her head and ran faster. Harder.

Amy felt a blister form on the back of her heel; she did not slow down to accommodate it. She pulled her watch to her face again. Astonished at the speed of her running, she silently thanked her mother for that gift. The sudden remembrance of her mother brought a whole rush of memories into Amy's consciousness, and Amy came to a direct halt.

She stayed at a standstill for several minutes, her blood pounding and her heart racing. The sky was stained with pitch, as if someone had thrown blue-black paint, the same color as her heart, over the sky and blanketed it in darkness. Amy looked up, expecting to see only a sea of misery blue, and she instead saw that the stars glowed with a different kind of light. They cast a sheer glow on Amy's face; Amy knew they glowed because her mother was there with them, no longer with her, but in the stars somewhere, glowing that different kind of light.

And Amy cried, for what she had left unspoken.

Ashie

by Rie Maeda, age 13

"**D**AD," I WHINED, stomping the sole of my new black riding boot into the hard pavement of the driveway, feeling my heel grinding into the small pebbles. "Can we go to the stable yet?"

I tugged on the handle of my dad's old pickup truck, yearning to open the door, hop in, and drive off.

"Ashlyn, honey, I'm just trying to snap the buckle on Amber's riding helmet. You're going to have to be patient."

I looked over at my dad who was wrestling with my ten-year-old sister, Amber, trying to wiggle the glossy blue helmet over her tight blond curls. Amber laughed and squirmed as my dad tried to buckle the little childproof snap on the helmet. Finally, Amber pulled away from both the helmet and my dad's grasp. She ran away screaming and giggling around the back of the house, her curls flying, her blue eyes sparkling, trying to find a place to hide. My dad stood there with the helmet and sighed. He looked over at me, shrugged helplessly as if to say, What can I do? and then ran after her, yelling, "I'm coming to get you!"

Rie was living in Lexington, Massachusetts, when her story appeared in the May/June 2010 issue of Stone Soup.

I sighed, leaning back against the cool window of the truck. I checked my watch. I had put on my own helmet exactly an hour ago. And now, I was going to be late for my riding class, all because of Amber. And wait a second—didn't this same thing happen last week? And the week before that? Oh, and yesterday Amber scooped up the last spoon of mocha almond fudge ice cream that I had already called dibs on and Dad and Meredith didn't get mad at her. And this morning, it wasn't an accident that she used up all the maple syrup on her pancakes, leaving none for me. I turned around and looked at my reflection in the glass window of the car. My straight chestnut-colored brown hair, my hazel brown eyes, and tanned skin seemed so blah next to Amber's little blond curls, glittering blue eyes, and pale complexion. Amber and I were on different ends of the spectrum. While I'm serious, Amber was exciting and funny. I'm smart, but Amber acts like a ditzy, cute ten-year-old. When Amber's in the room, all the adults kiss her and pinch her cheeks and coo over her. When I'm in the room, the adults ignore me, or they start including me in their horribly boring adult conversations about global warming or what muffins are on sale at the market. When Amber grows up, she's probably going to be an old, happy woman, her big house filled with friends and family who adore her and look up to her. I'm probably going to be the little maid who sits in the corner of the room, whom nobody is paying attention to. I'm always overshadowed by Amber.

I turned my back to the car and to my relief, I saw my dad streaking out around the side of the house, carrying a laughing Amber in his arms. He buckled her up in the back seat of the pickup and said, "Come on, Ashlyn. Hop in."

Finally. I pulled open the passenger door and sat in the leather seat. I leaned back and relaxed. I was on my way to my favorite place. The stable. When my mom died five years ago, I wanted to do something or have something that would make me feel connected to her. Out of his grief, my dad had hidden all of my mom's possessions so he wouldn't have to look at them. I didn't dare ask my dad about Mom. So, I asked my grandmother, who told me that Mom was a champion horsewoman. So, I asked my dad for horse-riding lessons and a pass to the local stable. My dad had been a bit hesitant at first. He didn't want to go back to the stable, or see horses. They brought back memories of him and Mom that he didn't want to see anymore. But Meredith, my stepmom, had coaxed him into letting me start lessons. Meredith is so sweet and nice. I can't see how that little devil sitting behind me is related to her. Then, I realized that the little devil was talking to me.

"Hey, Ashlyn? Ashlyn? Hello? Anyone home? Ashlyn?"

I reluctantly turned around to face her.

"Oh there you are," she giggled her innocent little laugh. "Were you daydreaming? I don't know how to daydream. Billy Morrison at school daydreams. It's so funny. The teacher calls on him and he's always daydreaming so he's not paying attention so he's always like 'what?' Do you think Billy Morrison is cute, Ashlyn? I do, he's so funny. And he likes strawberries. Daddy? Daddy? Can we get strawberries on the way home? The juicy red kind? Billy Morrison likes strawberries and I wanna be just like him and I wanna learn how to daydream like Billy and Ashlyn. Oooh—we're going to horseback riding! Yay! I hope Victoria lets me ride Dreamer today. I love Dreamer. Her mane is all smooth and shiny and Victoria lets me brush it. Do you think I'll be able to ride the advanced trail today? Do you? Do you? I hope so 'cause Victoria said I will be able to soon. What's soon? Is soon in five years? Or in ten? Or is it in one month? Or one week? Is soon right now? Daddy, I..."

I groaned, slipping back in my seat, slouching way down. I could still hear her voice from way down here, my ear to the leather seat, her voice rushing through the air all around us, sounding like an annoying little bird chirping.

"Dad, make her stop," I moaned. Oh yeah, that's one thing I forgot to mention. My stepsister is a chatterbox times one billion. Talking is one of her necessities like eating and breathing.

If there were a sport in the Olympics for talking, my stepsister would take not just the gold, but the silver, and bronze too. And what's worse is that her voice is just so absolutely annoying. It's sweet and airy and it always makes the parents squeal and coo over her. To the parents, Amber's a jewel. To me, she's a nightmare. She's like a little tic that clings to you.

My dad turned toward me and said, "Ashlyn, honey, sit up please. That's dangerous. And please," he said, lowering his voice, "Amber's just a little kid learning about the world. Let her talk. She just wants everyone to like her."

Little? Did he just call Amber little? She's ten years old, not four. She's only two years younger than me. And everyone likes Amber. Before, I was my dad's little star. And now, I reckon Amber is. She always steals all the attention. Oh and yeah, sure, Amber so wants to be like me. As if.

AFTER ABOUT the longest hour of my whole life, we finally arrive at Happy Horse Stable. Ignore the name. They're one of the top ten best stables in the country.

I jumped out of the car, relieved to be out of that little box I was trapped in with Amber. I ran over to Victoria, the owner of the stable.

"Victoria, I'm so sorry I'm late," I panted breathlessly. "I…"

"Yoo-hoo, Victoria," a way too familiar voice chirped. "It's me."

I turned around and had to jump out of the way to avoid knocking into Amber, who ran straight towards Victoria and into her arms for a big hug. Victoria laughed and lifted Amber into the air. She then put her back down.

"Well if it isn't princess Amber," Victoria bent down and cooed, sounding like a teacher talking to a preschooler. "What would you like to do today, darling?"

"I wanna ride Dreamer," Amber squealed, with a big angelic smile.

"Oh, all right," Victoria said kindly, "Come on, sweetie. Let's go get Dreamer." She lifted Amber onto her shoulder and they walked off around the corner of the stable, leaving me standing in the dried mud. I sighed and walked slowly into the stable. I walked over to Camila, my favorite horse. I had named her after my real mom. I stroked her long mane and she whinnied. I pulled a carrot out of my pocket, and held it out to her. I giggled as she crunched the carrot, licking my fingers, and tickling my hand with her soft velvety nose. I led her out of her room and out of the stable. I hopped on her and kicked her side. She trotted quickly through the spacious grassy pasture to where my class was being held. They were all huddled in a little circle, talking strategy.

"Ashlyn, over here!" my teacher, Marilyn, called, lifting her head up and beckoning me over to the circle of horses and kids. All the other kids lifted their heads and smiled at me.

"Hey Ashlyn!" everyone called. I smiled happily, feeling relaxed and happy. I felt like I belonged.

"Ashlyn, we're working on jumps today. And I was just telling everyone about that jump you showed me yesterday at private lessons. Since you are our star, can you demonstrate a jump for the class?"

"Sure," I said, glad to demonstrate my skills. I had been horseback riding for about four years and I was already the best rider at Happy Horse Stable. I had won five national horse-jumping competitions and my shelf at home was covered in medals, trophies, ribbons, and certificates. The stable was my second home. I turned Camila around and we trotted over to the jumping spot. I positioned Camila on the starting line. I leaned forward, seeing the jumping bar about twenty yards away. I anticipated the rush of air I felt as I jumped. As everyone watched, I dug into Camila's sides and she shot off. We shot off for about nineteen yards. Then, we took air, sailing high over the bar and into the air. I felt like a princess riding a unicorn over a high cliff and onto the other side. We slowly descended five yards away from the bar, hitting the ground delicately. I flushed with pride. There was complete silence. I began to panic. What had I done wrong? Suddenly, my class burst into applause, cheering and clapping, whooping and hollering. Marilyn's face was shining with pride. Finally, after about five minutes, the applause died off. I smiled with complete satisfaction. But then, my smile slowly slid off my face as I heard cheering in the direction of Amber's class. I looked over to see Amber on her horse, standing next to a miniature jump, which she had apparently just cleared. Her class was cheering and clapping. I could hear Victoria shouting, "You're going to be our next Happy Horse stablewoman!" My face turned grim. My throat tingled, like I was going to start crying. The pit in my stomach grew deeper. I had had it with Amber. There was going to be only one champion here. And that champion would be me.

THE NEXT WEEK at lessons, to my utter disappointment, Victoria allowed Amber to go with my advanced class on the advanced trails at Sunnapeak Woods, a large woods located next to the five-acre land plot of Happy Horse Stable. All it took from Amber was a hug, some smiles, and lots of giggles, and Victoria said yes. I groaned under my breath when Amber galloped up next to me and started chattering away about some new thing or another that had happened at school. I quickly started ahead of the group, galloping Camila over fallen trees, through the rough advanced trail. Roots grew up from the ground dangerously. I shivered. Even though the sun was shining brightly, it was getting a bit chilly. I wrapped my sweater closer around me and hugged myself into Camila for warmth. After another hour of riding, I approached a running brook about four yards wide. This was going to be a jumping challenge. I anticipated the flying feeling. At the signal, Camila shot forward and we sailed high over the brook. As we landed I felt that same happy feeling, a feeling that I had done something right. Then, I heard a voice from very near call, "Ashlyn? Ashlyn?"

I turned around and looked across the brook to see Amber

sitting on her horse right next to the water's edge. Amber smiled, delighted to see me. I moaned. She had followed me!

"What, Amber?" I cried exasperated. "What do you want now? Did you have to follow me? It was bad enough that you were even put in the advanced class group! You aren't even good enough to be in my group. You just charmed Victoria into getting into the advanced group! You've ruined my life! You took all the attention away from me! Look at what you've done!"

I gasped, clapping my hand to my mouth. Had I really just said that aloud? Amber's face closed in. Her bottom lip trembled. Her nose scrunched up. Her eyes filled with small pools of tears.

"Amber, I..." I started. "I didn't mean to..."

"Well, I'll show you," Amber said in a quiet voice.

She turned around and trotted off. I thought she was going to turn around back to the farm, but then about twenty yards from the brook she stopped, turned around, and positioned her horse. She dug in and the horse galloped off towards the brook again. I knew what was happening before it happened.

"Amber, no!" I cried. "No, Amber, you don't know how to jump this far!"

Her eyes were now more determined than ever. She was four yards from the brook, three yards, two yards, and then it happened. Dreamer's foot caught on a root sticking out of the ground. Her back leg twisted and she fell down, whinnying. Amber bumped off the horse and flew into the air, screaming. "Help! Ashlyn! Help!" she cried.

I jumped off of Camila and ran towards where Amber didn't land into my arms on land. The air carried her down with a big splash into the brook. She didn't come up. "Amber!" I screamed hysterically. "Amber!"

Then, to my relief, Amber's head poked up out of the water. She was panting and bobbing up and down. The current was picking up speed. Amber sailed with the water, down the brook, bobbing up and down, screaming.

"Swim to the side, Amber! Over to me!" I cried, running down the edge of the brook, bending towards the water's edge, holding out my arms.

"I can't swim!" Amber yelled.

I knew what I had to do. I dove into the cold water, not caring if I was going to be soaking or not. I swam quickly with the current towards Amber, the distance between us growing smaller and smaller. I grabbed her hand and pulled her close to me. Then, I swam to the shore. I pushed her up onto the shore and then pulled myself out, dripping and panting. We both sat quietly on the shore for a while, shivering from the cold.

"Ashie?" Amber finally broke the silence. I looked around. Who was Ashie? Amber tugged on my arm. "Ashie?" I looked down at her big blue eyes. I was Ashie. At that moment, I felt something I couldn't describe. I don't know. I guess maybe a mix of relief, joy, and compassion.

"Yes?" I said in a soft voice.

"Ashie, I... I love you," Amber said in a soft voice.

At that moment, I realized something. Amber and I weren't totally different. We both knew exactly what to say at the right time. I looked down at Amber, shivering, huddled in the cold. I put my arm around her and pulled her in tight. "I love you too," I whispered, so just she could hear. And there I sat, on the edge of a rushing brook, the grass moist with our drops, the sun shining through the trees, a slight breeze whistling through the forest, with my stepsister. No, actually, my sister, Amber.

The Strawberry Olympics

by Ryan Gallof, age 13

LOOKING BACK at this I realize how important Chad was and still is to me. I realized that he was no longer Chase's little brother, and was now my cousin that I loved, no, my brother that I loved.

I always loved going to Atlanta to visit my family. Well, mostly the Sittens. Let me rephrase that, I always couldn't wait to see Chase. The Sittens are my mom's identical twin's family. I loved hanging out with Chase, the oldest son. I saw him as an older brother more than anything.

My second mom, Aunt Kathy, suggested that we go strawberry picking at the largest strawberry farm in Atlanta.

"It's the biggest one in Georgia," Chase stated.

"Yay!" Chad shouts in joy and remembrance of his previous times there.

"Sure I'll go," I said.

That's when my mom starts giving out orders.

"OK, you get the sunscreen, you get the baskets."

Ryan was living in West Chester, Ohio, when his story appeared in the March/April 2007 issue of Stone Soup.

"Mom, they give you baskets there."

"Oh, OK, never mind," she said, sounding disappointed that she was incorrect, like a child on Christmas without gifts.

Then she forgot that disappointment and we were all happy to go.

I jumped in the back of the van right next to Chad. All he could talk about was how much fun we were going to have.

"We're gonna eat as many as we can. We're gonna see who can get the most in a minute, who can eat their whole basket the fastest. We'll call it, the Strawberry Olympics," Chad said so proudly to think of the name.

"Wow, that sounds so boring. Why would somebody think of something that boring?" Chase mentioned like he knew everything.

He didn't.

Once we arrived there and decided what game was first, we got our buckets and began picking. I decided that I was going to ignore Chase and finally side with Chad. Chad and I were going to coalesce for the first time. I was new to siding with Chad, but what Chad said in the car sounded like there was nothing more fun in the world.

"Dude, I'm leaving you kiddies. I'm not gonna play your stupid games. See ya," he yelled across the farm.

Chase went to go on and do his own thing.

At first I leisurely picked strawberries. It was a warm-up for the games. I went to put the first strawberry in my mouth and I had this mouthwatering sensation. It was like all the colors of the world were blurry and all I could see was a strawberry and picture how good that tasted. They were strawberries, decadent and juicy. At that moment I knew I was ready to compete.

"OK. Let's see who can fill up their basket first?"

"Fine with me. I just don't want you to cry when you lose," I exclaimed, assured of my victory.

I ran down the rows of strawberries picking as many as I could. I looked over just to see Chad doing the same three rows down. My confidence grew smaller every time I looked over, but I knew I could come through. Just at that moment I heard...

"Done!"

Chad had beaten me. I was upset for the loss but I kept my head up high for the next event.

"Now it's my turn to pick the event," I said, knowing that I had to pick an event that I knew I could win, otherwise I would be down two to zero. That was a margin I couldn't overcome.

"Let's see... How about whoever can eat the most strawberries in one minute. You up for the challenge?"

"Let's see who's crying after this one."

"Ready... Set... Go!"

The minute had started and I was eating away. I watched the clock carefully to make sure I was going to pace myself to not get too full and not be able to keep going. Then I glanced over at Chad. I saw he dropped one on his shirt and the juice from the bottom of the bucket was leaking all over his pants. I burst into laughter.

"Ha ha, Chad!!!!" I couldn't help but laugh at him not noticing that he looked like a giant, red strawberry himself.

Once he realized how much I was laughing he couldn't help but laugh. By this time the look on my face just made laughter and joy explode into Chad. I think he blew a bubble with his nose. He just couldn't control himself. (At that age everything was funny.) We both simply lay there with not a care in the world about who won. Now it was simply about having a great time.

We decided that the games were no longer needed to have fun. Even though Chase said that the games were dumb and we actually only finished one event he still wasn't right. So then we just sat there and enjoyed each other's company.

"I'm so glad you could come down."

"I know, usually we can only come during the holidays but I'm glad I got to come in the summer," I said, just happy to be near my family.

"C'mon guys," Aunt Kathy shouted as a signal to get us all in the car.

"Oh man!" we all yelled back.

We then all followed her to the car and thanked the owner of the farm as we left.

"I got the back seat," I yelled, hoping the louder I yelled the better chance I had of getting it.

"Fine, I got shotgun," Chase stated in protest.

As Chad and I settled in the back of the car I knew Chase was going to send a wisecrack my way.

And he did.

"So how was the Strawberry Olympics?" he says in a baby voice.

"It was so much fun."

"Yeah, we had a great time. Sorry you couldn't join us... not," Chad throws an insult at his older brother.

Chase sits, disgusted that he doesn't have a comeback. Chad and I just sit in the back of the car so happy that we could do something this fun.

"Dude, we should ditch Chase more often," I said.

"Ha ha, yeah man."

Chad and I just ramble on and on about how much fun we had. It was one of the greatest eye-opening experiences of my life. Not to mention one of the most fun. We continued to laugh and play in the back of Aunt Kathy's car until we got back to his house.

This one moment in time then, was only a fun outing. Now this moment speaks to my heart. I now realize how important Chad is. Now I don't just have one brother in Chase but two with Chad.

THE STONE SOUP BOOK

Rescue

by Mailyn Fidler, age 13

IF YOU HAD looked at us from above, we would have seemed like three ducks waddling out of our house and into the rain. My fat raincoat flapped at my legs, and my too big galoshes *clomp-clomp-clomped* on the wet pavement. I glanced nervously at my sister, who held clamped in her sturdy, pale hand a small plastic doll. My dad towered above us, like a tree in his heavy green coat and black cowboy hat.

After what seemed like forever, our sojourn down the driveway ended in a rushing river: the gutter. "Ready?" my dad asked, and we nodded. Although we tried to keep our faces solemn and stern for this grand event, tiny smiles peeped out from the quivering corners of our mouths. My sister opened her wet, slippery palm and dropped the doll slowly, almost reluctantly, into my dad's outstretched hand. My dad's body pivoted smoothly towards the gurgling gutter of water before us. Despite my efforts to restrain it, a small sound escaped my throat. "Are you sure you're ready?" Dad asked again. Swallowing, I nodded. My

Mailyn was living in Bloomington, Indiana, when her story appeared in the September/October 2007 issue of Stone Soup.

dad uncurled his fingers, and dropped the doll—*sploosh!*—into the surging stream.

For a few expanded moments, the water taunted us by pulling the doll slowly, teasingly away from us. I held my breath and kept my hands clenched tightly by my stomach as I watched the doll ease painfully through the eddies.

Then suddenly the rushing rivulet churned and swept the tiny figure away, down, down the street. The three of us broke into a run, galloping after it. With each step I took, a little of my anxiety for the doll disappeared. I flew down the sidewalk, drenched with the sky's tears. I skidded round a bend in the road. My hair, saturated with fat raindrops, flew around my face in strings. The doll shot down the hill in front of us, carried along by the churning channel of water. I hurtled after it, half-skipping, half-running. I was elated, happy beyond belief. A laugh rose from deep inside me, rising up through my throat. As it burst forth, I choked on it. My elation turned to terror. The image wavered in front of me, convulsing with my unsteady steps. A rusty, encrimsoned grate greedily gobbled the sloshing streamlet—just a few yards away! "Daddy!" I screamed. "She's going to go down the drain!"

Valiantly, my dad leapt forward, and brought his hand crashing down into the tumultuous waters. I squeezed my eyes shut.

A few moments later, all I could hear was the water cascading violently into the sewer. Cautiously, I opened my eyes. There, above the foaming jet of water, was my dad's hand, dripping wet, suspended over the drain. And nestled among his slightly curled fingers, outlined against the pale, soft skin of his palm, lay the small plastic figure of a doll.

The Dragon Speaks

by Emmy J. X. Wong, age 11

"**H**EY *new* girl," a boy's voice boomed large out of nowhere. "Are you Asian? Are you from China?"

Emily's face felt scorched. She knew it was turning the deepest shade of sunburn right now because she was dying of embarrassment. She slid further down in her seat, halfway under her desk. In her first week at her new school, this was the last thing Emily Chang wanted—to call attention to herself in this way. But she couldn't help it. It wasn't her fault.

"I'm American, just like you," she found her courage. Talking over the din of whispers in the room, she added in a small, barely audible voice, "Chinese-American," stressing the *American* part.

Emily quickly jumped up from her seat as the bell rang, signaling the end of her math class which had been her favorite class—that is, up until now.

Oh why did we have to move from San Francisco to Boston? she asked herself, but she already knew the answer to that tired and futile question. Dad had lost his job as a sous-chef at one

Emmy was living in Weston, Massachusetts, when her story appeared in September/October 2008 issue of Stone Soup.

of San Francisco's leading hotel restaurants and Yeh-Yeh (which means father's father in Cantonese), had offered him a job back home in his restaurant, the Golden Dragon, in the heart of Boston's Chinatown. Dad said they were "lucky that they had somewhere to go."

Yeah, right, she thought. She could feel her anger and disappointment surging again inside her, as she pictured liquid mercury rising in a thermometer stuck in a bubbling bath of boiling water. She couldn't squelch it this time. This time, the mercury was sure to win out and the thermometer would snap. She was at her breaking point. San Francisco was the only home she had ever known. She was born at San Francisco General. Although she had only been in her new home barely a month, she already missed the sprawling picnics her family celebrated in Golden Gate Park, their sauntering walks through the Palace of Fine Arts on sunlit spring days, dim sum each Sunday morning with Gung-Gung and Paw-Paw, her grandparents on her mother's side, but most of all she would miss her charter school and all it meant to her. At her old school, which was ninety-five percent Chinese-American, she didn't have to explain herself. Everyone there used chopsticks at lunch, knew how to write their name in both English and Chinese and didn't question why Chinese New Year was the biggest holiday of the year. Now in this new school she was assigned to, she was the only Asian-American student in most of her classes. She felt like a guest at her own birthday party. When Mom said it would take some getting used to, she wasn't kidding.

Emily hopped on the long mac-and-cheese-colored school bus and stole a seat in the back. She felt her head throbbing from the day's latest disaster and was happy when she started seeing telltale signs her stop was coming up. She eagerly awaited passing under the cherry-colored arch, the gateway to the city's Chinatown, to signal she was home. To her, it resembled an oversized Chinese character scrolled in the finest calligraphy. She smiled at the curbside phone booths fashioned in the shape of tiny pagodas, now relics with the advent of cell phones but quaint nonetheless. From her bus window, she could see a carefully arranged string of golden roast ducks hanging in the window of her favorite bakery. Some lucky family tonight would have a scrumptious meal of crunchy roast duck with soft plump bread pillows, the kind that melted in your mouth. Her stomach grumbled. She jumped off at her stop in front of Yee's enticing silk shop and rounded the corner, heading for her grandfather's restaurant. Her family of four, which included her mom, dad and little sister, Sabrina, had moved into the cramped apartment in Chinatown above the restaurant while Yin-Yin and Yeh-Yeh, her dad's parents, had moved to a roomier home in the nearby suburbs. She didn't mind their cramped quarters, so Dad could be close to his work. She loved being in the middle of all the excitement downtown. From her bedroom window she marveled at all the fascinating sights and delighted in the familiar sounds. Neon dragons and great walls turned on at dusk, illuminating the community's pride in their culture. She loved the glittering storefronts with all their shiny silks and hand-painted porcelains, and all the signs in Chinese characters she had no difficulty reading made her feel right at home.

Emily stood for a minute outside the jewelry shop and peered in. She admired the sparkling collection of jade pendants and rings. There were so many different shades and hues of the translucent gemstone. She knew that the deep emerald color was valued the most and she couldn't wait till her thirteenth birthday when Mom told her she could pick out her own jade pendant. She knew exactly which one she would pick. "Every girl needs lucky jade," she was overjoyed to hear her mother say.

Her excitement bubbled over, looking at the gold picture frames which hung in the window. These were the kind shopkeepers bought to congratulate one another when they had gained enough capital and courage to open their own shops. Thick gold characters, carefully framed, hung on a ruby velvet background, spelling out congratulatory wishes, such as,

"Wishing you good luck and prosperity in this new venture," and other things. Someday, she hoped she might even follow in her dad's and granddad's footsteps and open her own restaurant or gift shop. Then she might have her own lucky sayings.

Looking down at her watch, she knew she had a date to keep. She had promised to rendezvous with her family in the restaurant for an early supper before going upstairs to complete her homework, and before the customers would start coming into the restaurant, in droves!

One last stop, she thought. She was tempted by the incense-like scent wafting from the tea shop next door with some of the fanciest green and black teas from Hong Kong. They called out to her to explore, however that adventure would have to wait for another afternoon. But she couldn't keep herself from what was happening inside the expansive window of Calvin Chen's Kung Fu Academy. Pressing her face against the spotless glass, she saw the students of all sizes with long bamboo sticks, facing off against each other, ready to spar. Swiftly and decidedly they moved back and forth to a rhythm repeated thousands of years since ancient times at Shaolin's Temple. She couldn't wait for the colorful lion dancers from the same academy to win over the hearts of every visitor lining the streets come New Year's next week, as they had won hers watching them practice. Emily sped up and soon found herself in front of the Golden Dragon. She looked up to admire the deftly dancing dragon over the entryway. He wore a fierce expression, announcing to all he was someone to reckon with.

"I could learn something from you," Emily whispered to the wise-looking mythical creature. Inside, the music made by the clanging plates from the wait staff mingling with the air fragrant with soy and ginger made her feel more relaxed and welcomed. She slid into the familiar worn leather booth next to her nine-year-old sister, Sabrina, who was chattering nonstop. Sabrina wore her thick black shiny hair in a ponytail, which bobbed up and down as she told Yin-Yin all the events of her day. Soon Yeh-Yeh came out from behind the swinging silver doors which led from the kitchen, balancing two rounded bowls of perfectly cooked white rice and a plate piled high with Shanghai crispy noodles soaked in a savory beef sauce. The noodles were sure to keep Sabrina busy long enough so Emily could get some questions answered. Maybe she could ask Yeh-Yeh before Mom and Dad came out. She wouldn't want them to worry about her. She knew Mom would be hurriedly carving pink-and-white lotus flowers from radishes to adorn some of Dad's most delectable dishes, while he topped off sizzling signature dishes like Peking duck and firecracker shrimp.

"Yeh-Yeh, why did you come to America?" Emily began in a shaky voice, trying to steady it but wondering whether life back in China would be better than needing to explain yourself everywhere you went outside the limits of the city's Chinatown.

"Life in China can be very hard," replied Yeh-Yeh truthfully. He began his familiar story which Emily never grew tired of hearing. "China has been through many famines. I became a street vendor, selling little trinkets just to survive, and that's where I met your Yin-Yin. She had a street cart and made the most superb, freshest noodles you ever tasted. Every day, I would eat at her cart, sitting atop a barrel, and together we talked about our hopes and dreams for a better future. I fell in love with your Yin-Yin and together she and I knew we needed to immigrate to America for a better opportunity for our family. Now, I have two gift shops and a good restaurant that your father will take over for me."

"But, do you ever *miss* China, Yeh-Yeh?" Emily asked impatiently, not getting the answer she was seeking.

"Sometimes, but I have all that I need right here with me. When I miss China, all I need to do is look at your grandmother. She is far more beautiful than the rarest jade. The sound of her voice is more brilliant than the timbre of the most brilliant gong, announcing evening meal. Her spirit is stronger than the most upright bamboo and she is more flexible than... than... even these noodles in her ability to take on new challenges," he added, laughing at his latest simile. "I look at you and I see her," he added affectionately. "You have all the same traits as your grandmother." His thoughts were interrupted by the winter sky, lit up with scarlet streamers filtering in through the windows.

"Look there, outside the window. The dragon has begun to chase the sinking ball of fire and will continue to chase the ball of fire across the sky all the way to China," he murmured intently.

"Oh Yeh-Yeh, you can't possibly believe that. You know the earth spins on its axis and we are facing away from the sun now," Emily softly chided.

"Oh yes, I know that is the *scientific* explanation, but my heart tells me to believe what my ancestors believed. See, when I think of them and where I have come from, I am not so alone. I stand tall with pride and remember those who sacrificed before me, so that I could lead a better life," he resumed patiently. Emily blinked away a tear. Suddenly, listening to Grandfather's consistent and reassuring voice, she was not so afraid. She wondered if this is how Magdalena felt when she came to her old school wearing her striped fiesta skirt that her *abuela* had brought her from Mexico City to celebrate Cinco de Mayo, reflecting the same pride and colors as the Mexican flag.

Her grandfather's pride and his sentiments resonated that evening in her bedtime thoughts before she drifted off to sleep.

"As beautiful as the rarest jade, as brilliant as the gong, as strong as the bamboo, as flexible as the noodle," she repeated, smiling to herself. Yes, she could be as flexible as Grandma had to be moving to a new country and get used to her new school, even if it meant overcoming all the obstacles in her way.

"HEY AMERICAN GIRL," she heard bellowing across the room at her the next day at the end of math class. "Can I be your friend?" It was that menace Eric again, the boy who had taunted her only yesterday. Suddenly he didn't seem to bother her any more. She was proud of who she was and her family, all of them she had dreamed about going back many generations. She was

THE STONE SOUP BOOK

from a proud people, rich in culture and beliefs. She wouldn't hesitate again to own up to her Chinese roots.

"I'm not good at making friends. I have a lot to learn. I'm sorry that I said something to offend you, especially it being your first week and all." It was Eric now walking next to her out of class, trying to apologize.

"Why do you want to be my friend?" Emily asked.

"Because you're the smartest kid in math class and you seem really nice. I'd like to get to know you better."

"Well, it takes a big person to admit his mistakes," she replied. "I guess we can be friends."

"I'd really like that, Emily," he added with a smile.

"Emily? You know my name? What, no 'Asian girl' today?" she kidded amidst an easy laugh. Now it was his turn to blush to a deep crimson shade, the color of *hong bao*, lucky money envelopes given out every Chinese New Year to children or anyone lucky enough to receive them. Emily giggled. "I guess we *all* still have a lot to learn, and Boston is as good a place as any. I think I'm gonna like it here." Her heart sang. Somewhere she knew the dragon was also smiling. His heart sang too as he chased his golden ball of fire across the sky all the way back from China.

JuJu

by Natalie Schuman, age 11

JUAN (PRONOUNCED JU-AN) walked into our living room where my parents were sitting at the table. My mom and dad knew right away that she would be the one. She was wearing jeans and a Barbados T-shirt. She had brown hair, brown eyes, and brown skin. My sister, Emily, was two at the time and I was not yet born. Emily walked up to Juan and shook her box of Tic Tacs.

"You want one?"

Juan smiled and shook her head. "No thank you, Emily." Juan had a look on her face that said, *I think I'm going to like this kid.* Emily gave her the same look right back.

Then Juan sat across the table from my parents. When the interview was finished Emily walked up to my mom and said, "Mommy, I like that lady." She was only two years old but even then she knew that Juan was going to be our babysitter.

Juan took care of Emily until Emily was five. Then I was born and she would take care of both of us. Juan sat in the waiting room with Emily and then an hour after I was born she came in

Natalie was living in New York City when her story appeared in the July/August 2007 issue of Stone Soup.

and held me. I have a picture that the nurse must have taken for my mom of Juan holding me.

From then on Juan and I were as close as we could get. She sang songs to me like "Oh My Darling Clementine," and songs that she knew from when she was growing up in Barbados. Even now I remember her voice clearly singing them to me. I remember one day very clearly. We were in a park (I can't remember which) and I had stubbed my toe and was crying. Juan picked me up and sat us both down and rocked me like a baby. She sang those songs to me and it calmed me so much. Juan or JuJu as I liked to call her was like a second mother to me.

"How long do I gotta stay with you, girl?" Juan would often ask in a joking manner.

"Till college, JuJu!"

She would laugh and then kiss me on the head.

Our family always said that Juan knew our apartment building better than we did. Because later on in the years that she worked for us she was mainly alone in the house with our dog, she was able to do laundry and hang out with all of the staff that worked in our building. When she and I were going somewhere and we saw someone new that worked at our building Juan already knew their name.

"Hey Pablo!" she would shout from across the lobby. "How's the wife and kids?"

"Sharon is good, so are Benny and Samantha," the doorman or maintenance guy would say. Then they would pause a minute and be happy that Juan remembered. "How are Harry and Kenny?" (Juan's husband and daughter).

"They get by," she would say with that great smile. "See ya later! Stay sweet!" Pablo (in this case) would walk away with a happy feeling, while I would walk away feeling bad that I didn't know Pablo's name until then.

I used to, and still do, go over to JuJu's house for sleepovers. Juan and I play dominos there. She makes me barbecue ribs for dinner. She lives in Brooklyn so every so often Juan and I take the train to her stop and walk the couple of blocks to her house. Along the way we can't get a block without running into someone that we know. Juan will say hello and introduce me.

"This Natalie, I babysat her since the day she was born."

Her neighbor or friend would widen her or his eyes and say, "This is Natalie?" They would look shocked. "The one you don't stop talking about?" Juan and I would smile shyly. "Well," they would smile back, "it certainly is a pleasure to meet you." They would stick out their hand and I would shake it.

When we finally got to Juan's house we would relax and talk to Kenya, Juan's twenty-three-year-old daughter. She always had stories about college and questions about my school.

Soon Harry, Juan's husband, would come home. He was a doctor. He would ask me how I was and join the conversation. Then Kenny would go do homework, Harry would watch a baseball game or the news, and Juan and I would go into the kitchen.

I sat at the kitchen table while Juan made me drool with all of the great smells of her cooking. She would make the best barbecue ribs ever. She usually made peas and corn along with it too.

When I asked her once where she learned to cook so well she would smile and say, "I'm from Barbados," as if that would explain everything.

"I remember one day when I was about eight Juan and I were walking hand in hand on our way down the street. Two men stared at us with hatred.

"Why don't you take care of kids your own kind?!" they yelled at us. I could see a tear spark in Juan's eye.

"You don't talk like that to me and my girl!" Juan yelled back and just like that we continued walking, but in silence. Me being Caucasian and Juan being African-American never seemed like a problem to me but apparently some people really needed to grow up.

Emily and I just finished doing the dishes when our mom called us into the dining room. We sat down, thinking our parents were going to tell us the plans for the weekend. We were trying to be shocked when my mom told us that it was time to have Juan stop working for us, but we knew that this conversation had been coming up.

Juan had been our family's babysitter for thirteen years. She came to our house every weekday morning at seven-thirty and left at six o'clock to go to Brooklyn where she lived. She babysat my sister since my sister was two and now my sister is sixteen. We loved Juan and it seemed impossible to live without her. But the truth was that we didn't need her anymore. I walked to and from school by myself and went places after school with my friends. And my older sister did almost everything on her own.

The last day she worked with us was the saddest day of my life. I sat on JuJu's lap as she stroked my hair and told me that we would still see each other all of the time.

"Natie, don't you worry," a tear fell down both my cheek and hers, "I will always love you and I will see you very often." She held me tighter. Right then I thought about how she always asked me how long she would stay with me and about how my reply had always been till college. I always knew that it would never happen but I had secretly hoped she could.

But after all of that Juan was right. We see each other all of the time. She got a job babysitting in my building and I see her every morning and sometimes after school.

Juan will always be there.

The Summer Father Was Away

by Sariel Hana Friedman, age 10

"**J**O-BEAR, JO!" a voice called. "Wake up, wake up—it's just a bad dream."

"Where am I?" I awoke, puzzled, my eyes only half open.

A familiar face hovered over me in the morning light, sun-bleached hair strewn across his forehead, and clear glacier-blue eyes. A boy about fifteen—my brother, Nathaniel.

"Where are we going?" I questioned with a start.

"Crazy with Maisy and Daisy!" Mama said. That was Dad's favorite phrase—it meant that, as hard as we pushed, we would never pry it out of him.

Our father, Matthew, was at war. It felt empty the three of us in the car without him. For a long time I could only hear the forlorn sound of the wind and the rhythm of the tires on the dirt road.

"I wonder where Daddy is right now," I asked.

Sadness fell like a heavy blanket; I knew everyone was thinking about Daddy. I closed my eyes and imagined what he was

Sariel was living in Pacific Palisades, California, when her story appeared in the May/June 2007 issue of Stone Soup.

doing, but the pictures were blurry: maybe he was listening to the scratchy sounds of the radio as he tried to stay awake on patrol. Maybe he was cleaning his rifle, rubbing oil on the barrel the way he'd shown me. Maybe he was writing us a letter, his flashlight getting dimmer and dimmer as the batteries faded.

"We're here!" my mother said, her voice filled with an enthusiasm I sensed was a little too fake. I was jostled out of my reverie. Rolling down the window I could hear the faint sound of sighing waves. Bunny rabbits, startled by the rough engine cutting through the silence, stopped to stare, then run. The summer cottage father loved so much looked gray and forgotten. The flowers he had planted drooped, no longer able to find the light of day.

As we carried our bags through the door the sour scent of mothballs overwhelmed the comforting sea-salt smell of our summer home.

"Let's go straight to the beach," my mother called. "Come on, it'll be fun."

Nathaniel and I looked at each other—we both knew she was definitely trying too hard.

"The sun's not even out. It'll be freezing in that water. I'd rather stay here."

"Fine—then I'll just go by myself," my mother said, "and I'll bring those frozen Baby Ruths you love so much with me."

It wasn't because of the candy that we gave in; it was for Mom, it was for how hard she was trying.

I was pulled in our familiar red beach wagon down Tanglevine Lane next to vines of wild grapes. I was stuck between a mix of happy and sad, torn between two people, loving both equally. Mom was chattering away about who knows what until, finally, we arrived.

"Well, we're here," Nathaniel muttered, uncomfortably. "Er—might as well go in the water."

At first my brother and I jumped the waves dutifully, skin white with goosebumps. But, as the waves got bigger, so did

Nathaniel's spirits.

"Here comes a humongous one. I challenge you to dive under."

Breathing hard, I closed my eyes and prepared to dive.

Suddenly I felt comforting arms lifting me—up, up, up—then throwing me across the waves. Exhilaration!

I fell under the churning foam, the voices on the shore muffled. But I could hear my father's voice above the rumble of the waves, "No matter where I am, no matter what I do, I'll always hold you tight."

The thrill of it made me laugh out loud, the first time in six months. Even when I realized that it was my brother who'd lifted me up, and not Dad, it still made me happy.

Out of the corner of my eye I saw—or maybe I was just imagining it?—Nathaniel's lips (blue and chattering) curling up into a hint of a smile.

"Who wants a frozen Baby Ruth?" my mother called.

"Isn't it wrong to feel so happy?" I blurted out when we plopped ourselves into the hammock we had made summers before.

I looked at Nathaniel, his lips embedded in a thick layer of chocolate. I pointed and stifled a giggle. He flashed a quick, embarrassed smile, white teeth with chocolate frosting.

"I've been waiting to feel like this since Father left—but I didn't realize I could," I said.

"Jo-bear, get real," Nathaniel said.

"OK, maybe not since he left, but for a long time."

I felt my mother's fingers tuck my wet hair back behind one ear.

"You're my smart girl, aren't you?" she said.

The steady drumbeat of my heart, still pounding, rang in my ears. The hammock sighed contentedly as we swayed back and forth.

"You can't buy a day like this," Nathaniel announced. It was a phrase Father used that always made us laugh.

Before I knew it, he was pulling me across the beach on a boogie board.

"Faster, faster," I cried. This time, he, too, was cackling gleefully.

I remember that summer—way more than the rest: father returned with war stories to tell us (with occasional sound effects from Nathaniel). That summer was the turning point of my life. That was the summer I learned that I could live with sadness and still find a spark of joy.

The Forgotten Fort

by Andrew Lee, age 13

"**B**UT YOU'LL BE home to visit?" Ken looked hopefully at his brother, Tim.

Tim hugged Ken thoughtfully. "'Course I will," he said. "College won't be so much fun that I won't want to come back from time to time."

"I'm proud of you, son," said their father. "It's time for you to see the real world. Gain some independence, too."

Tim hugged his dad. "Thanks, Dad. I'll miss you."

Unlike their dad, who was broad-shouldered, lean, and stood with the best posture out of anyone they knew, Tim and Ken's mother was slightly shorter. However, she made up for it with her steely composure and deadly glare. Tim, who was once on the receiving end of many disapproving glances, was now wrapped in a kind, tearful hug.

"Now don't you get into any trouble," chastised their mom. "I don't want to hear any horror stories of late-night beer parties."

Andrew was living in DeWitt, New York, when his story appeared in the January/February 2009 issue of Stone Soup.

Tim made a face behind her back and Ken laughed.

"He'll be fine," boomed their dad. "Let the boy be. He can take care of himself."

Tim had his luggage close by. A backpack, one large compartment bag and a smaller suitcase with wheels. Tim had decided to "travel light," as their father had said, leaving many of his possessions to a grateful Ken.

The scene went silent for a moment, each person lost in their own thoughts of the coming departure. Suddenly, as the faint whistle of the train pierced through the air, Ken felt an overwhelming emotion overcome him. He and his brother had been through so much together. So many happy memories still lingered in his mind. Now his heart was giving way at the prospect of losing one of the closest people in his life.

The train creaked to a stop, and passengers stood up to board the train. Tim gave one last family hug and walked bravely away, not daring to look back at the tear-stained group behind him. The door slammed shut with an angry hiss, and the well-greased wheels of the train slowly began to turn. Tim's smiling features were plastered to the window, as his face was slowly carried away.

Their mother began calling frantically to the half-open window.

"Be good, you hear!

"Make sure to go to bed early!

"Don't forget your homework!"

The train gathered speed as it left the station. Tim had time for one last wave before he disappeared from view.

And that was it. Ken was left with a strange sense of loneliness, as if he had just lost his best friend. What would life be like now without Tim? He trudged wearily back to the van and climbed in. A light shower of rain was beginning to start up outside. The pitter-patter of the rain banged playfully against the car window, the streaming water distorting the image of Ken's face. It was a long ride home.

THE MORNING AIR was fresh and cool, carrying with it a faint trace of pine. Ken awoke sleepily, murmuring contentedly in bed as the chilly breezes blew in from his open window.

The night before, Ken had cried himself to sleep. It had felt as if he had been swallowed in a pit of sadness and regret. The morning came as a shock for Ken, and he felt as if he was losing his brother all over again. No one was there to fight for the bathrooms, no one was there for their mom to yell at, no one to have their sleep-deprived face blink tiredly at the breakfast table.

Ken had always been an early riser, and he climbed out of bed long before his parents had stirred in the bedroom down the hall.

He walked outside into the brilliant morning. The dewy grass brushed against his naked ankles, but Ken didn't care. The morning air was exquisite, and Ken breathed deeply, thankful to be alive on such a perfect day.

With no particular motive, Ken shuffled across his backyard with his Nike flip-flops. He gradually walked into the woods that he had spent so many years exploring with his brother. Familiar trees and half-built forts revealed themselves to Ken, dew hanging from the leaves like the tears on his own face. Ken cried openly in the woods, a place of solitude where he had his own privacy.

Finally, he rubbed his eyes and ducked beneath some vines hanging at the entrance to one of the long-forgotten forts. Three large rocks sat resolutely in the center, while the area was fenced off by fallen branches and dead sticks. Branches of pine needles were woven between neighboring trees to obscure the view and make it impenetrable to unwanted invaders. The dirt floor was ground neatly and removed of any tough roots, pebbles, or pinecones.

Ken ran his hands over the smooth rocks, remembering the laughter that used to emanate from the clearing, the countless hours that he and his brother had spent carefully plotting the fort. Their sweat was as much part of the fort as the trees themselves.

But somehow, the air was stiller than usual, quiet without his brother's voice to accompany his thoughts and feelings.

Ken was filled with grief, knowing that his brother would never come back to play with him in the fort that they had made together. He suddenly missed his brother so much that his heart ached with a longing for just one more day to spend with his brother. He realized that there was still so much he didn't know about his brother, and questions that he wished he had asked.

Ken took his walking stick that was still propped up against the rock and looked around for the knife. Carefully, he started to shave the stick of its bark, trying to complete his walking stick so that it would gleam white with the pale flesh underneath. Fond memories of lazy afternoons fluttered through his mind, reminding him of the long conversations that he and Tim had shared while carving their own walking sticks.

A sudden flutter of the branch above his head caused him to pause and look up. A bird with red feathers had plummeted to the ground, now waving its wings in a frenzied attempt to get up. Ken studied it carefully. It was barely grown, with a small beak, beady eyes, and a tuft of bright feathers for a tail. Ken could see that it had broken its leg.

"Poor thing," murmured Ken. "How did it get here?"

He looked up to see the nest, barely visible in the foliage above him. There were still a few broken shell fragments in the dirty nest. Its mother was nowhere in sight. Ken carefully picked up the fledgling in his palms, taking care not to cause it any more pain.

The bird obviously was not suited for flight yet. Ken wondered if it had been deserted by its family. With a sickening wrench, he thought of himself as a bird in the same predicament. With Tim gone it seemed like no one was there to guide him, to look after him. All his life, Ken could never have imagined what it would have been like without his older brother. The one friend that was always there for him, who even defended him against the bullies on the school bus. Ken wondered if the bird in his hand had a brother of its own. Where did its family go? He vowed that he would not let the bird die. Ken gently stroked the bird's head until its fluttering had slowed.

On impulse, Ken thought back to all the times his brother had taught him something or showed him something really cool. Tim's memory would always be here in the fort for Ken to cherish.

Poor little bird, thought Ken. He'll have to grow up without ever spending any real time with his brother. He cupped the baby fledgling in his hands and walked slowly back to his house. Don't worry, Ken thought as he blinked in the morning sunrise, making his way back up to the house. I can be your big brother from now on.

Saturdays

by Sophie Stid, age 13

To ELSA, SATURDAYS mean bliss. Saturdays are the morning of her entire week. They are the crowning glory, the cherry on the top of the sundae. A week without Saturdays to Elsa would be a week without happiness. She takes what she can get. And she gets Saturdays.

All week long, she taps her patent-leather-clad toes. She fidgets and she flutters. She doesn't have the patience to button her dresses or shirts, or zip up jackets. She's a blur, she's a nuisance. She's waiting for her Saturdays. Her parents smile fondly, and her sisters scoff. But what can they do? The brownstone at 23 East Hampshire Street is the kingdom, and Elsa is the miniature queen. Mother, Father, Clara, Heidi, and Tanya, they all jump to her commands. The eldest, Lena, does too. And can they help it? Just a frown from the little dancer casts a shadow over the whole day. Even Palinka, the brown-and-white dog, is devoted to Elsa. No treat tastes as good as bacon from Elsa's pudgy, dimpled hand.

Sophie was living in Menlo Park, California, when her story appeared in the May/June 2007 issue of Stone Soup.

Elsa's treats are Saturdays. Friday night she comes home from dance class, and plops her little four-year-old self by the dining room window. She sits, all by herself, in the velvet crimson window seat, and carefully lets down her bun of red-gold hair. She slips off her dance shoes and her scratchy tutu, and lets them fall to the floor like unheard whispers. The dining room is glossy, decadent, and dark. Books from the mahogany shelves brood over Elsa, thinking important thoughts. Elsa is a little scared by the picture of Great-Grandmother Marguerite that overlooks the window seat, who has the hooked nose of people who died very old a very long time ago. But Elsa has learned to look defiantly back into Great-Grandmother's flat brown eyes.

Elsa herself has bright blue eyes, like well-tended violets or pieces of spring sky the fairies forgot to collect. She has a little upturned nose sprinkled with cinnamon freckles, and soft pink lips. Her upper lip is dented with a little scar, from when high-spirited Heidi dropped her on the hearth. Elsa has never quite forgiven Heidi for that. But she loves Heidi anyway. Elsa is a person who loves naturally. Even Heidi, who is all long legs and jutting elbows and who can be hard to love. Some people can sing and some people can run, but Elsa can love.

Elsa leans her red-gold head against the mahogany paneling, and taps her fingers in a rhythm. She hears Clara practicing at the piano. Music fills the house like piney smells, grand and booming. Clara, who is fifteen, loves the piano. Clara wraps her whole soul in music, like a down blanket. She hums all the time, even in her sleep. When she walks home from school, her long gangly legs in their navy-blue-uniform tights skip to the tune of an unheard violin.

Elsa hears Tanya with Mother in the kitchen, banging oven doors, stirring, whirring the beaters. Heidi is groaning in the living room, angry with math. Heidi takes up so much space, with long legs and arms and wild auburn hair and flashing green eyes. She vibrates with contained energy. Elsa doesn't. Elsa radiates peace.

Elsa watches the people go by, bundled up and warm. They wave at her fairy image in the windowpane. She waves back, and then turns to Lena. Lena smiles at her little ballerina of a sister, bringing her cinnamon cookies. Lena stretches her lean arm along the mantelpiece, and lays her glossy brown head on it, and watches her sister.

"Elsie, how was ballet?"

"It was good." Elsa takes a deep bite of cinnamon-raisin cookie. "We did pliés. I'm to be a Snowflake in the Nutcracker."

"That's grand," Lena says. She smiles, her green eyes calm and comfortable, laughing at the little miniature witch of a girl. "And are you waiting for Saturday?"

"Oh, yes," says Elsa.

And then Mother comes in, moving quietly, a candle in her hand. "Elsie, *liebchen*, hand me the matches."

Elsa does so, scrambling, a little monkey in her tights. She hands Mother the box of heavy matches, and everyone watches as Mother lights the Friday night candles. Puff! The candles bloom like chrysanthemums in the darkness, Mother's hand shielding them from the wind.

SATURDAY MORNING ELSA wakes up early, and she lets twelve-year-old Tanya help her dress. Elsa buttons her red coat, and she takes her blue hat into Lena's room. Lena and Heidi are just waking up, fresh-faced in the early morning dawn. Lena brushes Elsa's hair, the brush sure and strong in her hands. She strokes Elsa's tangles into a red-gold halo of curls.

Elsa scrunches her blue tam-o'-shanter on her head, and Heidi frowns at her. Elsa smiles back, angelic and content. And then all the sisters walk out the door. They walk hand in hand, tall and dignified Lena, fiery tomboy Heidi, dreamy musician Clara. Plump and motherly Tanya holds hands with Elsa. One by one, they file into the corner deli. They get their bagels, they get their lox. The owner smiles at the Saturday morning regulars, and hands them free moon cookies.

Elsa hates moon cookies, but she wouldn't have any other cookie for the world. She licks off the brown-and-white icing, careful not to mix the two. She waits to lick the brown icing until all the creamy moon part is licked off, and the hard, tasteless half-cookie is slick and shiny in her mittened hand.

The sisters walk to the park, and eat the bagels there. Elsa's heart is singing and dancing. She thinks her chest might burst open with how happy she is. Lena smiles at her, thinking her own private thoughts. That Elsa. Always staring at something in the distance, something that pleased her and made her rose-pink lips twist in one corner.

"Keep your fairy lands, Elsie," Lena whispers.

Elsa eats her moon cookie.

They walk all over Boston on Saturdays, a fresh-faced sight straight from Sweden. Old women smile, old men ask wise Lena for help in their sidewalk chess game. Elsa and Tanya scatter crumbs for the pigeons, and Heidi balances on the fences. Clara taps her long skinny fingers, sounding out tunes and melodies on walls and trees and fence posts.

By three o' clock, they are always at the launderers. Billowy sheets piled in tubs, drying in the scent of lavender. The atmosphere is fresh and clean, warm and dry. The laundress fetches the laundry for the Olsons, asks after their parents. She hands each of them, even seventeen-year-old Lena, toffee from the caramel-warm basket on the counter. The waxed paper slides off, and the slick shiny candy melts on your tongue like afternoon sunlight. Elsa holds a bag of laundry, and wishes she were old enough to carry her mother's clothes. The silk and taffeta dresses, the net and sequined shirtwaists, the velvet feathered opera capes. Lena carries those. Heidi is not to be trusted with her father's suits, so solemn Clara holds the crisp black-and-white ruffled cummerbunds and vests. Heidi, like Tanya and Elsa, carries socks, pinafores, and the girls' checked gingham dresses in a laundry sack.

From there, they go to Nightingale Park. They lay the laundry

THE STONE SOUP BOOK

out on the grass, and they amuse themselves. Clara lies on the sunny grass with some sheet music, and Lena sews and Tanya mends. Heidi runs around the fountains, with Elsa on her back, skipping on the marble, her skirts flying up. She runs and Elsa screams in laughter until both are too tired.

But there are other things to do. There are swings, and there is the newspaper man, and there is the cigarette man, and there is the chimney sweep. Elsa runs and plays and explores every nook, every cranny. She plays with rocks as fairies, and she makes wildflower wreaths. She drinks in the grass and the lake and the sun, and this feeling. She sits, still clean, in the midst of a golden light. Nothing bad can happen today. Not today.

At five o' clock, it is time to go home. But on the way there, they stop by the carousel. Elsa's favorite part! The music and the painted horses, going up and down, lights like around a movie star's mirror. They arrive, and the ticket man looks up from the paper.

"Sorry girls, not today. It's broken."

Broken! Elsa's bottom eyelids fill with tears. Her lashes are glued in triangles, her lips tremble and bow.

"Elsie," Lena says, bending down, but Heidi moves her out of the way.

"Elsa," she says, taking the small girl's hands. "Elsa, we will have our own carousel."

Elsa looks up. The golden light did not protect her. "Heidi..." she sobs.

"We will," Heidi says firmly. "Climb on my back."

Elsa does. Then Clara gets into the spirit of the thing. She takes out her penny harmonica and begins to play "Waltz of the Flowers." Lena begins to dance, the bending and twisting and extending her ballet-cultivated body, up and down, up and down. Tanya sings along.

And they proceed, the Olson sisters, in their own carousel. And so it goes, the Waltz of the Flowers, all the way home.

Zachary

by Adanma Raymond, age 12

As MEL PICKED up the phone, my freshly bitten fingernails dug into the wooden carvings that decorated our antique chaise lounge. But the look he gave me after a few seconds made my heart sink for the gazillionth time that evening. Why weren't they calling? As he hung up the phone, Mel let out a long, long sigh. "It was Ms. Connelly, she wants to know if we have her ladder still, go and check won't you?" Mel's voice sounded bored.

I was about to leave our living room when the phone rang once more. This time, there was no disappointment on Mel's face.

"Dad!" cried Mel. "What's going on, is Mom OK?" Before my father could answer, I was on the kitchen phone shooting out questions a mile a minute.

My father's hearty laughter boomed from the phone, "Your mother is fine, children, and so is your new brother, Zachary."

I swear that when I heard those words, the sky lit up. My new brother! A long eight months ago, our parents had told us that

Adanma was living in Trinidad and Tobago, West Indies, when her story appeared in the March/April 2007 issue of Stone Soup.

THE STONE SOUP BOOK

we should expect a new addition to the family. Since then life seemed to drag, waiting for my new sibling. And now, now he was alive, a new child in the world. My brother.

Mel revved up his red Honda and we were on our way to the hospital. I sat in the front seat, looking out of the window and imagining my new brother. Zachary would have lovely, chocolaty brown skin, with jet-black curls sprouting up all over his head. He would have sparkling brown eyes, and rosy cheeks. He would be a gorgeous baby. He was mine.

"Mom!" I ran into the hospital room excitedly.

"Sam! Sweetie, come look at our Zachary!" I turned around and there, in my father's arms, was the most adorable baby I had ever seen. He was just what I imagined and more. His long, black eyelashes quivered as he blinked and began to stare at me. Tears of joy streamed down my cheeks as my father offered him to me. I agreed, and held out my arms. His soft body was now cradled in my arms and he looked up at me and chuckled with his small little mouth. Too scared of dropping him, I handed him back to my mother who smiled at me warmly.

"Don't worry, you have to get used to holding a newborn."

I played with Zachary for a bit and then the nurse said my mother had to do some tests, so did the baby.

We were about to leave when I felt something tugging on my finger. It was Zachary's little fist. I turned to him, with tears in my eyes and whispered, "Don't worry, I'll *always* be there for you."

A Long Way from Home

by Emily Livaudais, age 11

As KATIE DALE looked out the window at the icy tundra, she wondered about many things. She wondered what the surprise was her grandma talked about so often. She wondered if she would make new friends. She wondered what her house was going to look like. She wondered if it was possible to learn a new language in approximately three days. She wondered if all these thoughts were usual when going to a new country. Katie sat in the taxi frozen with fear. She was all alone ready to start a new life in Iceland.

Katie had been under so much pressure since both her parents died. She had been around almost all of America looking for a new family. Katie didn't understand it. Why couldn't she stay with her grandmother, why? Katie knew perfectly why, it was because everyone thought her grandmother was a crazy old lady who ought to be locked up forever. Katie strongly disagreed with this, but how could she change what was in the past? She was just thankful she was going to have some parents around to

Emily was living in Fenton, Missouri, when her story appeared in the March/April 2007 issue of Stone Soup.

THE STONE SOUP BOOK

support her.

"Here you are, miss, at the Akureyri Airport," said the taxi driver.

Startled by this remark, Katie paid the taxi driver a little of her money that was left to her by her parents.

When Katie stepped out of the car a sudden wind blew her leather bag off her arm and onto the ground. Her belongings spilled everywhere. She quickly gathered them before the wind blew them away. She was putting away what she thought was her last item, until she saw a white envelope marked Katie. She had never seen this before, but she recognized the handwriting as her grandmother's. She read the letter aloud in a sort of mumble.

My dear Katie,
I don't know if you will miss me on your long excursion, but I'll miss you terribly. I am so very proud of you leaving your home, and going far away with no support. But that is not true my dear. I always feel as if you are right next to me, and no matter what, you will always have me for support. I once lived in Iceland for nine years. During those years I made many friends. There is one friend I know that you must meet. Her name is Marrisa. She lives in an old antique shop fairly close to the Akureyri Airport. Enclosed is a ticket. In order to meet her you must take this ticket to the person behind the counter at the shop, and ask for Marrisa. If he is kind enough he'll let you take her home with you forever.

With love, Grandma

P.S. I'm sure your folks won't mind Marrisa living with you.

Katie was so happy to know her grandma had friends right here in Iceland. She immediately started looking for the antique shop.

Katie wandered not far into an odd little shopping town. She looked and looked in every store window. Finally she saw an old building full of many odd things of different shapes and sizes. This must be the store Grandma mentioned in her letter,

Katie thought.

As she entered the shop a sudden burst of warm air hit her in the face. There were racks with candlesticks, paintings, mirrors and dolls. Straight ahead was a counter with an old man behind it. Katie walked up to him and handed him a small golden ticket. The man looked puzzled, until Katie said, "Marrisa." The confused look on the man's face faded.

He also spoke English, and he said, "She's downstairs between the lamps and jewelry."

Now Katie was puzzled. The man, then, took her by the hand and led her to a small dark room below the store. He led to a part that had shelves full of old broken things that Katie couldn't tell what they were, except one thing. It was the most beautiful doll she had ever seen. She had a very detailed face, and she wore a blue dress with 1684 embroidered at the bottom. Katie stared at her for a long time. The man must've noticed, because he took the doll off the shelf and handed her to Katie while saying, "This is Marrisa. There isn't much I can do with her, but you can have her for free if you'd like. I got her from an old friend of mine. I knew her for nine years."

Katie didn't know what to say. She just nodded her head and turned to walk back up the stairs. She was near the top of the staircase when she looked back at the old wrinkled face and said, "Thank you," in a soft gentle voice.

Katie walked back to the airport feeling just a little different than before. She easily found her parents, because they held up a sign that said Katie.

That night Katie found some paper, and wrote:

Dear Grandma,
I met Marrisa today. You were right, the man let me keep her. Since I got her I've told her everything. She's like my new best friend that I can always trust. My parents are great, they even speak English. They live in a cozy cabin near a huge forest.
I love you a lot, Katie

As Katie curled up in her bed she thought to herself, I have two great parents, one best friend, and a grandma who loves me. How could life get any better?

A Different Kind of Lullaby

by Meg Bradley, age 13

HER ROOM was quiet. Too quiet. In fact, the whole house was quiet, and Abby knew why. It was empty—all except for her. There had been a note, of course, there was always a note, waiting on the table after school.

> Abby:
> Gone out for a while. Be back soon.
> Love always, Mom

Abby wondered why her mother couldn't have been a little more specific, and exactly what her idea of "soon" was. That had been approximately three o'clock, now it was around ten o'clock. She lay in bed, tossing and turning. The silence scared her; it seemed to envelope her and swallow her up. The quilt made her too hot; she pushed it off. Now she was shivering; she pulled it back on.

Abigail means "father's joy," she thought angrily. If I was his joy, then why did he leave us?

Meg was living in Dubuque, Iowa, when her story appeared in the January/February 2007 issue of Stone Soup.

THE STONE SOUP BOOK

Groping around in the dark, feeling for the right buttons, she turned on her radio, turning it up as loud as it would go, blasting it through the house, but the emptiness remained inside her no matter what the volume of the music. She eventually turned it off, but found that she could not lie still, could not take the silence any longer.

For one fleeting moment, she screamed, her lungs burning. It made her feel a little better; the screaming gave her an odd sort of sense of power. The feeling only lasted a moment, though, as her common sense took over—what if someone had heard her? What if they had called the police? The fire department? What if one of the neighbors came over to see what was wrong? What if someone called Social Services when they found out she was alone? What if... What if...

She had to keep herself from thinking these things. Come on, Abby, focus. Green meadows, blue skies, calm river, tweeting birds... She played the game she and her father had played so many times, when she had stage fright before a school performance, envisioning the perfect place, but this time it only served to make her more agitated. Oh, Dad!

Swinging her legs out of bed, she got up and walked over to the window. She shoved it open, desperate to hear those nighttime sounds that would fill up her room with reminders that summer was not far off. A gust of warm wind rushed in, sweeping back Abby's long chestnut hair. Crickets chirped their evening song, an occasional lightning bug flashed, then receded into the darkness, flying away to new and better things. How desperately Abby wished that she could do the same.

She slammed the window shut with a deafening crash that reverberated against the walls, and then the room was once again quiet. She only heard the bang as if from a distant place, vaguely felt the cold glass beneath her hands, felt her fingers sliding down, down, down. Just how she felt. Her world was going down, down, down.

Abby gently leaned her head against the windowpane, trying

to fight the emptiness swelling deep inside her. She wondered what had happened to those times, so long ago, when her mom and dad had sung her to sleep, familiar lullabies, beckoning her to dreamland, step by step. Although she knew that at twelve, many people would consider her too old for lullabies, she still missed them achingly. The soothing sound of her parents' voices had always filled up the silence that haunted her now.

Lullaby. Even just the word was soothing, like someone stroking her hair, holding her hand. Like a hug right when she needed one.

If I ever needed one, she thought angrily, it's now. Parents, guidance counselors, teachers, they always say they'll be there for me when I need them, but where are they all now?

Abby flung herself face down onto the bed, drowning her face in her pillow to muffle the heart-wrenching sobs that she was sure could not be hers. Gradually, her back still rising and falling, the sobs began to come more softly, in a certain rhythm, a certain pattern, and she began to relax. Her breathing began to come easier, and she drifted off to sleep at last, to a different kind of lullaby; the feel of hot tears running down her cheeks, the sound of her own ragged breathing, her own crying. Her lullaby.

IT WAS MIDNIGHT. Abby knew that she must have fallen asleep at some time, because she had just woken up. She put out her hand and felt her pillow—it was still damp from her own tears. She heard the sound of a car pulling into the driveway, heard her mom come in and get into bed. Abby resented that her mom had been out so late without even specifying where she was going, but she knew that her dad's leaving must have been just as traumatic for her mom as it was for her, alone in the master bedroom, in the queen-sized bed by herself. Even with her mom back in the house, Abby could not shake off the emptiness, and she felt a strange tug inside when she realized that her mom had not come in to say goodnight, as she always had before.

Desperately she insisted to herself that there must be a way to make the loneliness go away, she just hadn't found it yet. Suddenly something her English teacher had told her class just the day before came rushing back.

"Poetry can be therapeutic," Ms. Stevens had said. "Write what you feel. It'll make you feel a lot better afterwards, I promise." The kids in her class had moaned and groaned, saying they would never in their lives write poetry of any kind, but Abby had tucked away that information for future use, thinking there might be a time when she needed something like that.

Abby flicked on her bedside lamp, and reached for a pen and paper. Maybe Ms. Stevens was right, maybe she wasn't. There was only one way to find out. She grabbed up the pen and began scribbling frantically, crossing out, rewriting, crumpling the page, and starting over again until she was finally satisfied.

The lights flicker off,
I listen, but all is quiet—
too quiet.
Where are those days
when someone would sing me to sleep,
gentle notes
luring me slowly to dreamland,
filling the silence,
my lullaby?
Nothing
can cover the emptiness
like the sound
of someone singing,
sweetly singing.
I open the window
hoping to hear the sounds
of the summer's night,
but no chorus of crickets chirping
no soothing warm breeze
or flicker of fireflies

can mask the feeling in me,
take away my fears.
I hear
as though from far away,
the window slam shut,
feel the glass
beneath my hands,
and I cry myself to sleep—
a different kind of lullaby.

She read it, and then again and again. Ms. Stevens had been right; she did feel better, much better, as if a huge weight had been lifted off her shoulders. A poem. In a sense, it too was a lullaby, just as her tears had been. But this kind of lullaby helped her give names to her feelings; let her know they were real, that maybe even somewhere there was someone else who was experiencing the same thing. Maybe she would show it to someone, maybe she wouldn't. Not yet, anyway. She wasn't ready quite yet. It was *her* poem, her lullaby, one only for her.

Love—A Cursed Blessing

by Akash Viswanath Mehta, age 10

Introduction

FIRST OF ALL, you must know that my story is not unique. It's merely the same tale as millions, maybe even billions of human beings; a few thousand hearts broken every day the same way as my life was shattered. Shattered but able to be put back together, piece by piece.

But keeping that in mind, this narration is not a happy one. It was the worst thing in my short life, and that life was in a ruin for a while. They say that for every good thing that happens, a bad, awful, miserable thing appears in the same story. Same story, same life. That's the way they say it. But I take it the other way. I say the opposite; for every bad thing a good thing appears. I am not responsible for my life, my story, but no doubt I have changed it—after all, a writer is the owner, and the *changer* of his book, is he not? Change. A meaningful word, and rarely used correctly. Change makes things what they are; change creates, preserves and destroys *everything*. Everything except change itself.

Akash was living in Brooklyn, New York, when his story appeared in the July/August 2009 issue of Stone Soup.

I have made up a phrase, and it is one of the few things to say and not be heard, only understood. "In every darkness shines a light within it." That simple sentence is so complex because of its truth. I believe that in every life it is prominent. It is there, and in the light in the darkness there is another darkness, a smaller but darker one, in which there is a tiny but dazzling light, in which another even smaller darkness... and so on.

But my story is not just light and darkness. It is also love and the breaking of love. It is, to name the affliction that blessed my life, my parents' love that broke, and when the love broke, the people broke apart from each other, and that led to the *creation* of many things, including a small baby who is now almost fifteen months, a love between five people that could *never* be broken, even if the previous time my mother had a love that could not be broken it broke. I am sure, with every atom in my being, that the love we have now will be whole forever.

Before I embark on the specifics of my tale, this must be known: I do not know, nor want to know, all of what happened in my parents' marriage that made them miserable. I assume I will find out in later years, and tears will fall from my eyes again, and the grief that I had will be reborn, though I do not know if it will be greater or smaller than my grief when the breaking of the love appeared in *my* life. Because the love had broken before I knew it, but I was unknowing, and ignorance was a blessing. But sometimes I noticed small things, which leaked out like a hole in a faulty pipe, and I wondered. Thankfully, however, my small mind passed those things over without a second thought. But they were still there, and unknowingly I was scared.

Chapter One: Before

M Y FATHER had been working on his book for as long as I could remember. In total, it took seven years. Much more time than he had been allotted by his publishers. The book had somewhat shaped my early childhood, and if not that, it had somewhat shaped my father, and of course, I was shaped by my father tremendously. I remember clearly, how he used to sit there in his study all day, how after school I would come home, go to his office, talk to him about my day, and then I would leave, and he would be there for the rest of the day, and he came out at dinnertime, and he would cook, and I would eat, and I would talk, and then go to sleep. In the time after I had my after-school chat with him and before my dinner, I would be with my mother. We might go to a movie, or work on an art project, or go to a park, or do whatever activities a mother does with a child. My father would be uninvolved, and I would wonder what he was doing there, in his study, working all day. But of course, I know now. He was making money, the money which bought me an elite private-school education, the money that paid the health insurance, the day-to-day money that bought me ice creams after school, the money that paid the babysitter, the money that bought my clothes—all the expenses were bought by him sitting in his study, working all day. And often he would go on trips to places around the world, to India, the place where his book took place, for as long as two months. I remember how I and my brother tried to Scotch-tape the door shut, to stop him from going, and the Welcome Back signs we used to make for him. You see, we loved him. He was not very involved with the family, but we loved him just as much as any son could love a father. And yet, we were scared of him. He was frustrated with money, and money was what he had to sacrifice everything for, and money was a curse. And he had a temper, because a man who is frustrated with what he does, who finds life so hard, a man cannot keep all those rages bottled up inside him. He got mad, and we silently got mad too, but we were too scared to voice our anger. But we didn't know the reasons, we didn't know how hard life was for him, we didn't know how much he loved us and how much he did for us, and we should have known. But we didn't, and anger grew, fear collected. But when I say "we" I mean me and my older brother, but I cannot speak for my mother. My mother knew things that I didn't and I don't, and my mother had reasons which I don't know, and my mother was my father's wife, and I was only his son, so obviously I wouldn't know.

In the few months before the dreaded divorce, my grandparents came over from London. Quite a few times, I and my brother were told to stay upstairs and play—apparently "adult talk" was happening and I was too young to hear it. I didn't know what they were saying, so I didn't mind the instructions. Once I needed to go to the bathroom, and when I went downstairs I didn't understand what they were saying, but I remember very vividly my grandfather's voice asking, "Do you love each other?" No wonder I was scared.

Chapter Two: The Divorce

MY FATHER was going to finally release his book to the world! And finally he was going to be involved with the family, finally he was going to be a great dad, finally everything was going to be all right. That day I had come home from school—but why wasn't I picked up from school by my mother? That was how it always was! Instead it was my grandfather, the same one who had asked that accusing question that made no sense. When I asked my grandfather why he was picking me up and not my mother, he told me that she was sick, and she wouldn't even be able to come to the book release.

I don't remember the party that well, all I remember was that there were so many people, all for my father. I was happy, as I should have been, but I didn't realize that it was my last time feeling truly happy for quite a while. Because when I came to my mother's home that night, I realized it was my mother's home and not my father's. At first, I thought it was a joke. Then I wept, and then we all slept in the same bed, crying throughout the night.

But wait. You have to think about how my father felt. He'd

spent the last seven years leading up to this day, and it turned out to be the most miserable of his life. He'd toiled harder than you can imagine, he had sacrificed seven years of his life for it, and the same day he had released his book, he divorced. And maybe you can see, now, what the family was. A father who had given everything he had for a day that turned out to be one of the saddest of his life. Two children who have just been thrust into a world full of fights and agreements and lawyers, whose life had been suddenly broken like a thin pane of glass. And a mother who had just voiced her rage over all the years, with no steady hand to guide and calm her, with two children to take care of. And then, everyone blamed themselves. My father said it was his fault, he broke the marriage, my mother said that it was she who had called the divorce, it was she who had finally said no, and my grandparents said that it was they who had convinced my mother. And then, there was me. Just imagine, for a moment, what it must have felt like. It is hard to put my emotions into words. I felt that I had done something terribly wrong, that I had made a mistake that cost my parents their love. And everyone was right to blame themselves, because it was all of their faults, except mine. I didn't do anything wrong. In fact, I couldn't do anything wrong. Because I was a small little boy whose most terrible act was innocence.

Chapter Three: Fights

I AM GOING to make this chapter short, as it is very painful to recall these events. But you must know what happened. After the divorce, my parents would have split apart, never talking to each other again. They would have never seen each other again, never communicated again. But I and my brother were the tie between them. We made them talk, and fight, and write to each other. Because they were both our parents, and there was an awful word that applied to law that they had to discuss. Custody. The word is used for prisoners in jail who have to serve a sentence behind bars, the word doesn't show someone's life—it only shows who *owns* the person. Reminds you of slavery.

This was the main fight. When were we at my father's house and when were we at my mother's. Who owned us, and when did they own us? Custody. I and my brother felt as if we were trapped between the two, my mother and father. We were almost like translators, going to one house and saying, "Amma (mother) says this..." and then getting shouted at and then going back to my mother's house and saying, "Pappa (father) says this..." and it would go back and forth. I cannot express how terrible it felt.

My mother wanted primary custody, my father wanted joint custody. My father won. A schedule was made, which luckily allowed me to see both my parents every day. One thing I am glad of is that my parents never had to go to court. The lawyers were there, they did fight, they did hate each other, but they never had to stand in a box and accuse the other parent of being an awful parent in front of a judge who would decide my fate. Thank God.

But it wasn't just fights between my parents, who were always fighting for me. Sometimes *I* fought—because really, it isn't my mother's time or my father's time. It is *my* time.

Chapter Four: Losses

M Y PARENTS DIVORCED. So obviously, the world was screwed up. Obviously there were losses. And yet, I didn't lose anyone. No one died, no one left, except the love between my parents. My mother lost her marriage, and she lost some (but not all) of the people on my father's side of the family. I lost being a child with two parents, having a normal life. Also, life is harder because of our commute—we spend so much of our time on the subway. My father lost the relationship that made him a husband. While these losses were permanent, and made a huge impact on my life, they're not the whole story.

THE STONE SOUP BOOK

Chapter Five: Gains and Benefits

MY MOTHER REMARRIED to a wonderful man called Stephan. He loves me and I love him. And my mother and Stephan had a baby named Satya. I love Satya just as much as I love my older brother. I have never used the term half-brother for him, and I never will. What an awful name half-brother is. So I gained more than you can imagine. Stephan has a lovely family which is my family too now!

And my father. As I have already said, before the divorce he was uninvolved with the family. My father's book was very successful. He won many awards, and the book has been published in many languages, and life is good. Most importantly, the divorce lifted a weight from his shoulders that was bigger than the new one it gave. He is a true father, and I love him more than ever. He spends so much time on things that are only for us—his entire life is based around us. He cooks for us, he takes us all around the world, he takes us to plays, he talks to us—he is a full father.

Chapter Six: Present Time

I AM TEN YEARS OLD. I was six when my parents divorced. You have read the story of my parents' divorce. I haven't gone into detail, but hopefully you get the impression. But now, things have changed. My father is a professor, living in a twentieth-floor apartment in the middle of Manhattan. He is currently writing his second book, this time about New York. My mother is the executive director of a nonprofit organization that helps people with AIDS. She just moved with me, my two brothers, and my stepfather to our new home. My older brother is a teenager. That explains it all! My younger brother turned one year two months ago, and is basically the cutest being ever to live. And I am a ten-year-old boy, who just finished writing this paper.

The Old Farmhouse

by Shannon Halpin, age 12

THE FARMHOUSE was small and old. Its ancient yellow paint was peeling from the clapboard walls. Its black roof was worn and was missing some shingles and sagged in the middle, as if an elephant had once slept there.

"I know it's not perfect but it just needs a few homey touches," my mom said, getting out of the car behind me.

"A lot of homey touches," I said huffily, dropping my bags on the ground.

"This is all we can afford to live in right now and I know it's hard on you and I'm sorry."

We unpacked in silence and when we were finished I sat drinking a cup of juice sulkily at the kitchen table.

"Why don't you go find something to do?" mom said, putting a box of cereal in a cupboard.

"Like what?" I said gloomily.

"Go exploring."

"Fine," I said angrily, getting up and heading for the door.

Shannon was living in Bow, Washington, when her story appeared in the January/February 2007 issue of Stone Soup.

"Janie?"

"What?"

"Don't forget a sweater."

"Whatever!" I said, grabbing a sweater off a chair and shoving it over my head. Then I strutted out of the house, slamming the screen door behind me.

I heaved at the barn doors and they slid open. The first thing I noticed was the smell. The stench of rotting hay and dust filled the air and I sneezed. The barn was also dark.

I fished my flashlight out of my pocket and turned it on. That is when I realized how big the barn was. It seemed to stretch a mile back. On one side four stalls clung to the wall and on the far side a ladder led up to a hayloft.

I headed to the ladder and examined it closely for loose or missing rungs. Surprisingly, it was almost perfectly intact. I climbed up into the loft. Nothing was there, only a few moldy hay bales.

I climbed down the ladder and started to investigate the stalls. They were all the same: same bins, same moldy hay covering the ground. Just as I was leaving the last stall, something shiny caught my eye.

It was a doorknob. I tried it and it opened. I cast the beam of my flashlight into the opening and saw stairs leading down into the earth.

"Mom, Mom!" I yelled, running back to the house, forgetting about my anger about the move for the moment. Mom came running out and looked relieved to see I was OK.

"Come on, I've got something to show you!" I called.

It was a long walk down the stairs and it was freezing by the time we reached the bottom and I was glad I had brought my sweater.

A small room was at the bottom of the stairs and Mom said, "Wow, this is really old. People a long time ago might have lived down here during storms. That is probably what it's for."

I had remembered my anger and was being quiet again.

"This can be our own secret place," she said, putting her arm around my shoulder and squeezing me close to her. In that moment, I felt my anger evaporate completely and it was replaced by guilt. I realized I had been very selfish and had only been thinking about myself. The move had been as hard for her as it had been for me. Then I did something I hadn't done in a long time. I looked up and smiled at her.

A Faraway Place

by Emmy J. X. Wong, age 11

NAN STARED DIRECTLY into the gray fog, letting the present day obliterate into the cold ethereal wetness. Standing defiantly on the pitching deck of the fast ferry, the *Flying Cloud*, which had left Hyannis only one hour earlier, she stared blankly at the emerging and unwelcoming, rocky shoreline in front of her and the cream-colored moorings that dotted the horizon fast approaching. How could her mom do this to her? she questioned. She was referring to her mom sending her here, or was it... nowhere? How could her mom send her to the place the Native Americans called "that faraway place, Nantucket"? she asked herself. It just wasn't fair. "She knew what summer vacation meant to me," Nan declared stubbornly. Nan relived the worn-out argument she had had with her mom at the ferry terminal just before her departure. She didn't want to understand why she had to take care of Grammy Armstrong in 'Sconset for the whole summer while her mom stayed behind to work as a nurse at Cape Cod Hospital. She and her mom had moved to Cape

Emmy was living in Weston, Massachusetts, when her story appeared in the May/June 2008 issue of Stone Soup.

Cod, Massachusetts, less than a year ago, just after the divorce. Her mom had said she wanted them to be closer to her family. Little did she know then she'd be sent to take care of an aging grandmother she hadn't seen since she was five years old! "It's not fair," she heard her pleading words now echo aloud to an unsympathetic, weathered seagull who had come to perch on the cold, steely railing next to her. "I won't see any of my friends this summer." But no one was listening. She thought about the stolen sleepovers she and her new best friends, Molly and Claire, had carefully planned, the lost trips to sandy white beaches under azure skies that the Cape was famous for, and the lazy days she had planned to bank reading beneath the generous awning of a shady maple in the backyard before starting seventh grade.

Just then a single blast of a horn sounded to interrupt her reverie. "Prepare for landing," she heard the captain's voice bellow across the crackling loudspeaker.

The auburn-haired girl pulled her nubby, evergreen sweater tighter around her waist and wiped away a tear before finding her bag and departing down the gangplank with a crowd of tourists. When she reached solid ground, Nan dutifully pulled out her cell phone, dialed her mom first to tell her of a safe arrival, then the cab company owned by her uncle. In no time at all, a cheerful man of few words, simply dressed in a khaki pressed shirt and a sea captain's hat, Uncle Tommy of Tommy's Taxi, had scooped her up and headed for the eastern part of the island where she would spend her entire summer totally bored to death, no doubt.

When Nan arrived at the natural shingled two-story clapboard Cape on the leeward side of the island, she was immediately taken by the ruffled carmine-pink roses that grew in sprays from bushes hugging the bleached-shell driveway and the lacy blue hydrangeas in the front garden. The sunlight was peaking out from behind the clouds, now casting a cheerful wash of sunshine over everything in her path. She stole a quick glance upward at the black iron weather vane forged into the shape of

THE STONE SOUP BOOK

a whale, which sat atop the roof, and wondered if it held any special significance. Upon entering the house through the side entry, Nan was enveloped by warmth that felt as comforting as her mother's old calico patchwork quilt she used to drag from the hallway closet whenever she was sick. There was a familiar feeling to the place. Nan headed up the uncarpeted narrow steps to the breezy second-story bedrooms where Uncle Tommy had promised she would find her gram, before he had to hurry off to pick up a paying customer.

Immediately upon eyeing the frail woman with the dancing pale-blue eyes and mop of snowy hair, Nan knew she was home. "I'm so happy to see you, my Nanette," exclaimed the older woman, with enthusiasm. "I hope I won't be a burden to you," she added meekly, her voice withering. "Ever since I caught pneumonia last winter, my Yankee stamina just hasn't been the same." Nan hugged the elderly woman firmly and returned a wide grin. She was genuinely happy to see her gram and hoped she would be on the mend soon. She now wanted to be of some help to the sprightly woman she felt close to but barely knew.

The next day, Grammy Armstrong was sitting up among the patchwork covers and working her hands to create what looked like a neatly woven basket. "It's a lightship basket," she informed Nan. "My great-granddad was a lightship keeper in the early days, as were many in my family."

"What's a lightship, Gram?" asked Nan with keen interest.

"A lightship is like a lighthouse, only it's a ship that floats offshore to keep sailors from crashing on the shoals," she began to explain. "These waters south of Nantucket are some of the most dangerous seas you'll ever come across. Hundreds of ships have wrecked in these parts, so the lightship was the answer to warn sailors in the south shoals." It seemed Nan now had more questions, not fewer, after her gram's studied reply.

"What's a shoal? But how is the basket related to the lightship? Do lightships still exist? Can I go see one?" Nan anxiously fired back a flurry of questions.

"Come with me," Gram beckoned, taking Nan by the hand and leading her downstairs to take up a comfortable corner in the warm, sunlit kitchen. Over steaming mugs of peppery Earl Grey tea and sweet raisin scones lavished with heaps of tangy rose-hip jelly, Grammy Armstrong told her tales of lightships and stalwart Nantucket whalers. The whole time, the older woman's leathery and freckled hands never stopped weaving the lightly colored reeds to fashion the most beautiful basket Nan had ever seen. Nan thought Gram seemed delighted to share her tales and the apt skill she had perfected over her lifetime making the highly sought-after baskets prized by both locals and tourists alike.

Nan's time on the island soon became a string of lazy days spent in the backyard staring down at her brown hands and arms which had been gingerly kissed by the summer sun as she gleefully but industriously worked her baskets. She didn't even mind the necessary interruptions by her frequent bike trips into town to pick up Gram's medicine at the small pharmacy atop cobbled Main Street, which also gave her a chance to window-shop at the local toggery or sample some of the "world's yummiest fudge" at Auntie's Fudge Shoppe next door. The days of summer soon flew by faster than the *Flying Cloud*, like they always do, and Nan was surprised how quickly she had picked up the art of making the elegant but simple baskets. "It's in the genes," Gram Armstrong had whispered to her one day, "just like the salt in the air," she grinned. "Your great-grandfather was a whaling captain who built this home, and your grandfather was a shipbuilder on the mainland in New Bedford."

Nan smiled back. Soon it would be time for Nan to return home. She cherished her time on the island. Her favorite pastime though had become her beachcombing excursions when she used the smallest of her baskets to carry her treasures home, including perfumed saltwater rose hips, heliotrope bivalves and glassy pebbles. She was content here and experienced a sense of belonging that she had never known before.

When it was time to say her goodbyes, Nan was happy to see

THE STONE SOUP BOOK

her grandmother looking so high-spirited and healthy. The lilt had returned to her laugh. She had apples in her cheeks and she was able to get up and move about the former whaling captain's house more agilely. "Come back next summer, and bring your friends with you, my Nanette. Now that I am back on my feet, I could use your help restoring Sankaty Head Light." Nan let her thoughts drift to the well-known landmark nearby and the pride she felt in the light with its signature red and white stripes. Her daydreaming however was interrupted by the kindness in her grandmother's melodious voice. "Or you and your friends could hunt for relics for the whaling museum." Nan pictured the prominent edifice standing tall at the end of Steamship Wharf that she had marveled at when she first arrived. "You were named for this island, you know," she heard her grandma shout after her as she entered the familiar yellow taxi. "It's in your blood."

Nan looked down at the sturdy, rounded lightship basket carefully perched on her lap that she and Gram Armstrong had lovingly woven together at the start of the summer, which was now taking on a caramel patina. Nan thought about her savored trips to the local beach only steps away, the cool ocean waters lapping eagerly at her sun-baked shoulders and the welcomed salt spray that cooled her tanned face and made her rusty curls coil more tightly. She would miss this place. She had loved her quick jaunts to the shoreline to watch the rainbow fleet bob merrily by, engined only by the refreshing westerly winds. It had been a great summer and the best part of all was time spent listening to her gram's stories about her family's lore as keepers of the lightships and making beautiful baskets to while away the hours. Smiling to herself, Nan knew her gram was right. She would come back to this faraway place. Maybe someday, she might even call it home.

The Animal Kingdom

by Mackenzie Hollister, age 12

CLOUDS LOLLYGAGGED across the sky, carried gently by the occasional half-hearted gust of wind. The sun, giving its all for that clear sunny perfect day we'd been hoping for, was defeated by the humid cloud that seemed to swallow up all of Pinckney, Michigan. We were left sticky and disgusted but somehow satisfied with the green grass that had finally replaced the snow. Sounds like any old April day, right? Ha! That's what I thought too. If I could have predicted the future then, I wouldn't come back to this memory, my last good memory with him, every other night in my dreams. If I could undo everything now and relive it over and over again and never feel anything but the feeling I had then and there, I'd be happy. I would be honestly happy for the rest of my life. Yeah, if I could undo everything and erase the unwanted, everything would be fine. But I can't, and it's not.

You see, it started as just another one of my trips to Michigan to visit my crazy, gotta-love-'em family. Mom was hustling around, neatly stuffing all of the essentials into suitcases. Dad

Mackenzie was living in Newton, Massachusetts, when her story appeared in the July/August 2006 issue of Stone Soup.

THE STONE SOUP BOOK

was doing what she told him to. Fluffy, our cat, was lying on the suitcases, effectively protesting our departure. And I was going through a mental list of everything I needed and always forgot: alarm clock—check; riding jeans and sneakers—check; underwear—check; hair towel—ooh… the hair towel—check. It was all normal. Things still proceeded as normal from the taxi ride, to the plane ride, to the two-hour car ride to my grandparents' house in Pinckney, Michigan.

When we finally arrived we were greeted with hugs and kisses from my aunts, cousins and of course my grandma and grandpa. There, and only there, my mother finally relaxed and got prepared for sleeping in and no cooking. I was happy too for I was at my favorite place in the world. What could be better than to be spoiled, loved, always have something to do, and be surrounded by cousins? Days in Michigan were always laid back: sometimes we would go to Screams, a Halloween-themed ice cream store appropriately placed in Hell, Michigan; other times we would ride horses, go to the lake, or just hang out and be with each other. I guess it didn't really matter what we did, as long as it was with the people we loved.

The first day started like it always did in Michigan, at seven thirty, to the TV news and laughing voices of my grandparents. I tiptoed down the squishy-carpeted steps like I always did and snuggled into my spot in my grandpa's lap. Then after a minute, he started drumming his fingers on my knee, like he always did.

As the day proceeded, my newly crowned four-year-old cousin came over and was excited to see me, her magical cousin. After chasing her around for half the day and laughing a lot, I was tired and the humid air got me feeling stickier than a melted popsicle, but no, Katie wasn't tired. At that point I dragged her over to where my grandpa was sitting drinking some ice water on the porch and I gave him a look. He seemed to receive it correctly as "Help me!" because he looked at Katie and asked her if she wanted to go on a picnic. I watched and smiled as her little blue eyes widened and her jaw dropped.

I followed her into the kitchen where we packed some crackers and pop in a little wooden basket with a quilt. We then tromped back out and met my grandpa where he was standing, turning off the electric fences that contained the horses.

We started walking past the barn—a place filled with happy memories of horseback riding. Inside I could hear hoofs hitting the ground, music playing and my aunt singing along. We kept walking into the pasture where Peaches and Misty, the large, beastly, gorgeous inhabitants, munched on their evening hay, and down the long hill to the back of the pasture, farther and farther away from my grandma who I could still see in the bright kitchen happily making dinner. I had never been that far back in my grandparents' property. I asked him where we were going but he just said, "You'll see." I laughed and looked over at my little cousin who was smiling and looking very excited. We kept walking, past the compost pile and the garden, past the little heap of junk that we never got around to cleaning up, farther and farther into the silence broken only by the occasional chirp of the crickets.

We finally ducked under a broken part of the fence and entered a new world, our world. Katie called it the Animal Kingdom. There weren't many inhabitants: just some bunnies, a gopher we expected by the hole, the occasional deer, and some bugs. You might think that it was generous to call it an animal kingdom but that is what it was.

In our kingdom we found a broken metal chair that looked like it had been sitting there for years, obviously of a long, royal, mysterious past. That would be the throne. We also found some ducks, a mommy and a daddy, that would be the king and queen. You might say it was nothing special, just a grassy spot on the edge of a secret duck pond, sheltered by trees and high grass. Forgotten and taken over by the bugs. But it wasn't, not to us. We loved it.

Katie loved the bramble bushes, which, if you were willing to get scratched a little and push aside the branches, revealed a

THE STONE SOUP BOOK

top-secret hideaway. I loved the beautiful spot. Grandpa loved us, and we all loved being there... together.

We had our picnic on the edge of the hardly-a-pond pond that disappeared in the winter and during droughts. While we were there we laughed, talked, and enjoyed each other's company. Being able to relax and let go was amazing, but to me what we did was insignificant compared to the people I was with. It was special then but not as special as it is now.

It was a good memory but we never knew it would be our last good memory.

Not long after I returned to home-sweet-home in Massachusetts, we got a phone call with some news that I still haven't fully accepted. My grandpa was diagnosed with pancreatic cancer—a very fast, mysterious, deadly cancer. They tried everything: alternative doctors and medicine, special diets, strange devices believed in some cultures to heal, bubbly foot rub supposedly godly and curing, healthy salt, and a trip to Mexico to a special healing center. It was all just for hope.

We visited him a little while after that animal kingdom trip and he didn't look the same but I knew he was still in there somewhere behind the sunken eyes, pale face and skinny shapeless body. He was always fighting. He didn't say much but what he did say I will never forget. He didn't want me to. He said, "Grandpa loves you." He kept telling me that.

Everything happened too fast for me, just a blur. All I could do was sit back and watch as everything just happened, even though I didn't want it to. It was like an emotional, sad movie that I watched from afar. Except I wasn't watching the movie; I was in it and it wasn't a movie, it was my life.

On July 15, 2005, the worst happened. I flew to Michigan again. This time nothing was normal: no mental checklist, no average plane ride. Just a solemn journey, spent looking out the window, to somewhere I wanted and didn't want to be more than anything. It was a hard week that droned on forever, with everything seeming to happen sluggishly slow; even my memories of that time are in slow motion. It was hard sitting in the first pew of a funeral service, and the first car in the funeral procession, but most of all it was hard holding an all-of-a-sudden cold hand.

In the lengthy speech I gave at his funeral I tried my hardest to explain the concept of the animal kingdom for Katie, who was too little to come. I knew she wanted everyone to know and so did I. I managed to talk fluently, calmly and I didn't mess up at all, which is hard to do at a time like that. But I did it for my grandpa. And I was glad I got up there in front of everybody because they all cared about him and had similar memories.

The whole town was there. My grandpa was one of the most loved men in Pinckney, Michigan. He was a builder, a township supervisor, a friend, and a great family member. I'm proud to be remembered as my grandpa's granddaughter. And I am thankful that I had that memory of him.

Katie and I still go down to the animal kingdom today and sit and remember our grandpa. Being in our special spot, talking to our grandpa, is the closest we can get to him now.

Sitting there listening to Katie look up and talk to him, mumbling, "I know you miss your little girl... can you ride down on your winged horse and visit?" is a new memory I have from that spot. When she saw the hot tears welling up in my eyes she whispered knowingly, "It's OK, he'll always be in our hearts."

Lying in the tall grasses, thinking to myself as Katie still rambled on, smiling at the sky, I realized something that I will never forget: sometimes you don't know how good you have it until it's gone. Right there with the hot July air suffocating me I learned one of the most important things I know: savor your animal kingdoms for you never know what the next day will bring.

The Garden

by Emma Agnew, age 13

THE LATCH CREAKS gently as I push open the gate. In front of me, a small potting shed covered with wild roses blocks my view. But I already know by heart what lies beyond. And sure enough, as I walk around the corner of the shed, the sight of a familiar garden greets my eyes.

But it isn't just any garden, it's *my* garden. Even though anyone can come here, it has always seemed to belong just to me. It has been my sanctuary in times of sadness and my inspiration in times of joy. But most of all, it has always been somewhere where time seems to melt away: where there are no math papers due, no people to be polite to, no mothers to get into fights with.

Everywhere I look, a perfect tapestry of color and shape greets my eyes. Here, perfect rays of sunlight reach down long fingers to gently caress the silvery leaves of a grove of aspen trees. There, a vibrant butterfly gently alights on the lip of a delicate blue-and-gold flower, slowly fanning its wings, anticipating its first sip of nectar.

Emma was living in Topanga, California, when her story appeared in the May/June 2006 issue of Stone Soup.

I breathe in deeply, inhaling the mingled scents of rose and hibiscus. Slowly, I can feel the anger coiled tightly around my heart loosen its grip. The memory of my most recent fight with my mother starts to fade.

For the past few years, our fights have become more and more frequent. Sometimes I feel like just flinging open the front door and running away. Usually I resort only to *slamming* the door. This time was just one time too many, that's all. I couldn't face her anymore. I had finally opened that door and left.

At first, my intention was to leave and never return. But now I wasn't so sure. The garden was having its usual effect on me: putting the jumbled thoughts in my head back into place, sorting out the tangled knot of anger and confusion I felt inside. No matter, I thought. I won't let myself think about that right now.

As I venture deeper and deeper into this garden of miracles, I come to a small bridge adorned with horsetails on either side. Instantly I am transported back in time to when I was six.

My Mama and I walk hand in hand over this very bridge.

"Wait, Mama!" I say, bending over. "I want to see the fishies!"

Mama lies down on the rough wooden planks next to me, and we both spend the next ten minutes immersed in the activities of the fish. When we sit up again, slightly stiff and sore, Mama reaches out and pulls a horsetail toward her.

"Look!" She says with as much excitement as if she were the one being shown this small miracle for the first time. Gently, she pries the sections apart and lays them on the wet ground next to her.

"Now, watch!"

Carefully, she picks up each piece and fits them together again. I can feel my eyes bugging out of my head!

After a few minutes of labor, she holds up the horsetail exactly as it had been before she picked it.

"Ta da!" she exclaims proudly.

As my memory fades, I can feel my eyes start to swim with unshed tears. Even though sometimes I feel as though I hate her, I

know that inside I will always really love her. Even though sometimes I want to slap her, I know that inside she will always be that
same Mama who showed me the horsetails, all those years ago;
and that I will always be the same little girl who clung to her hand
and exclaimed over the fishies' activities.

For better or worse, she is my Mama, and I love her.

Roaring Regret

by Michael Scognamiglio, age 13

SOMEONE'S TRUST can take years to gain, but only seconds to lose. Revving the motor of my best friend's dirt bike always gave me a thrill. Yet, nothing could compare to the feeling of zooming down the back roads by my beach house on a warm, summer day. As I switched gears from first to second, I glanced at an old woman giving me a cryptic stare. I saw her shake her head as if to say this was not safe, which only enticed me to go faster. I shifted to third gear and sped past her garden. I did not care about her opinion, for at that moment, going thirty miles per hour, I was the king of the world. The warm wind whipped through my hair while my shirttail flapped furiously in the breeze. Little toddlers venturing to the beach gazed at me in awe. Nothing could bring me down on that day... except for a small strip of gravel on the side of the road.

My head was up in the clouds so I failed to notice the sliver of sand and pebbles ahead. I plummeted down quickly from Cloud Nine, however, when I flew through the dusty air and onto the

Michael was living in Saddle River, New Jersey, when his story appeared in the May/June 2006 issue of Stone Soup.

hard pavement. I heard my friend stop his bike short, dismount, and rush towards me. Wanting to look cool in front of my fourteen-year-old friend, I stood up, brushed myself off, and forced a smile. He gasped as he pointed toward my arm. Suddenly I felt a flash of pain travel up my arm. I stared in disbelief at the blood dripping onto the bike from the dirty gash in my left arm. Gravel was jammed under the flesh of my palm, and my hip and legs were badly scraped. Holding in my tears of agony, I slowly drove back to my house and said I'd call him after I got cleaned up. After he drove around the corner, I sprinted through the front door and screamed for my mom.

To be honest, I had never told her that I was riding this motorized vehicle. So, when she questioned me, I simply told her I had fallen off my bike. She took me down to the ocean and carefully washed off my scrapes and cleaned the gravel out of my hand. The salt stung my open wounds. When she had finished, I limped over to my friend's house. I was feeling terrible, not just because of my injuries, but because I felt guilty. My mother had recited over and over how dangerous dirt bikes were and that I was never to ride them. The thrill of the ride clouded my judgment, and I did not heed her warnings.

Later that evening, we all went out to dinner. My sister had been with my dad in town during the day and was unaware of my injuries. So, when I was scooping up my lobster ravioli she noticed the cuts on my arm. She questioned me about the cuts and my mom replied that I fell off my bike. She misunderstood and thought my mom had said dirt bike so she blurted, "You fell off the dirt bike! Aha! Jesse said that thing was extremely safe!"

My dad chimed in with, "How did you fall? You looked like you were great at riding it when I saw you!"

My mom glared at me.

Watching my mom's face, realizing that she had been misled, was sheer agony. Her words, "I see you conveniently neglected to tell me the whole story," felt like daggers in my heart. Suddenly, as I looked at her face, I realized that trust was a very fragile thing. Her eyes clearly told me that I had lost her trust. I always knew she would forgive me, but I still regret hurting her because of my need for speed.

Not Ready

by Aubrey Lawrence, age 12

"MOMMY, NOOO! Don't make me go!" I clutched the leg of my highly embarrassed mother as she tried to calm my fears. It was my first day of preschool and I was terrified. I began to cry even harder when my mom attempted to pry me off of her leg. She told me that she'd be back *very* soon and that my teacher was *extremely* nice, but I held fast. I was unconvinced. The other little children stared at me with wide eyes as they witnessed the scene I was making. It wasn't pretty. My face was stained with tears and they continued to stream down my reddened cheeks. After a great deal of coaxing, encouraging, and bribing, though, I too was sitting in a little plastic chair inside a room that I was sure to be tortured in. The entire afternoon I refused to fingerpaint, eat a snack, or sing the alphabet.

As I SAT at the kitchen table a smile spread over my lips and I had to laugh at the old memory. It was hard to believe that the little four-year-old girl had once been me. But deep inside

Aubrey was living in Hinckley, Ohio, when her story appeared in the November/December 2006 issue of Stone Soup.

that was really how I felt, unwilling to leave my mother and detach myself from the familiar lifestyle I had lived for so long. I didn't want to take the next step. I knew that I had to, though. It was only another turn on the winding road of life.

Making my way to my bedroom, the room I had loved for so long, I let out a heavy sigh. When I reached the doorway I was taken aback. There, sitting on my bed, was my mom, my hero, and she was sobbing. I slowly crept to her side and tried to comfort her trembling form but soon found myself weeping as well. We cried together for a while, and it was my mom who gathered herself first. She smiled at me, squeezing me close. I returned her smile through my tears, glancing over at my packed bags and large bundles. I thought about college. What would it be like? I dismissed the thought, all that I wanted now was the comfort of my mother's arms.